PLANET JANET

Books by the same author

Confessions of a Teenage Drama Queen

My Perfect Life

PLANET JANET

Dyan Sheldon

PLEASE NOTE
GLOSSARY FOR THE UNINITIATED
IN THE BACK OF THIS BOOK

CANDLEWICK PRESS
CAMBRIDGE, MASSACHUSETTS

Copyright © 2002 by Dyan Sheldon

First U.S. edition 2003

Library of Congress Cataloging-in-Publication Data

Sheldon, Dyan.
Planet Janet / Dyan Sheldon. — 1st U.S. ed.
p.   cm.
Summary: Sixteen-year-old Janet Bandry keeps a diary as she deals with an
annoying family, school, a quirky best friend, and trying to find herself
through vegetarianism, literature, romance, and her "Dark Phase."
ISBN 0-7636-2048-3
[1. Family problems—Fiction.   2. Interpersonal relations—Fiction.
3. High schools—Fiction.   4. Schools—Fiction.]   I. Title.
PZ7.S54144 Pl 2003
[Fic]—dc21   2002073626

4 6 8 10 9 7 5

Printed in the United States of America

This book was typeset in M Joanna.

Candlewick Press
2067 Massachusetts Avenue
Cambridge, Massachusetts 02140

visit us at www.candlewick.com

For Erika T
and with special thanks
to Gayle Donnelly

THURSDAY 21 DECEMBER

Talk about self-centered! Me! Me! Me! Me! **ME!** That's all
anybody in this house cares about. I was trying to have
a normal conversation over supper (the way people do in
films, etc.), not some Great Intellectual Discussion (I know
my family's limits, believe me), when I realized that
no one was listening to me. I stopped dead right in the
middle of explaining about what happened at lunch (which
was v dramatic and emotionally stressful), and no one so
much as glanced my way. Sigmund (my male parent) was
messing around with his electronic organizer, as per usual,
and the Mad Cow (my female parent) was staring at him
with her eyes squinted like she was trying to work out

whether or not he was going to blow us all up. Also as per usual, my parents' OTHER child was reading some book like the rude, antisocial boil that he is. (Tomato sauce was dripping down his chin in a particularly revolting way. You'd think at his age he'd at least be housetrained.)

Anyway, I just sat there watching them for a few seconds. They were chomping away like lions round a dead zebra, oblivious to anyone but themselves (for a change, right?!!). And it suddenly hit me not just how Spiritually Alone I am, but how easy it would be for me just to GIVE UP and become like them: shallow . . . superficial . . . more boring than asphalt. I recovered from this DEVASTATING realization and asked them very sweetly if they were aware of the fact that I was trying to have a conversation. I'd've got more of a personal response if I'd farted. Still staring at Sigmund, the Mad Cow asked him did this mean he was going out again tonight and, still staring at his organizer, Sigmund said he was just checking his schedule, and was that a crime now or something? I could tell that they were about to start another fight, which is pretty much the only thing they do together lately. If you ask me, it's just as well Sigmund's hardly ever home, or the flat would be like war-torn Beirut or one of those places. So, for the sake of Peace, I cleared my throat and tried again. "Hello? Hello?" I shouted. "Is anybody there?" Which was when Justin suddenly looked up and made his one joke about Planet Janet trying to communicate with Earth. That, of course, caught the parents' attention. The three of them laughed like a pack of demented hyenas.

It's **TOO MUCH**, if you ask me. I'm at a v crucial time in my life when I should be encouraged to express myself and explore my feelings and experiences, and what do I get instead? I get, ooh, Planet Janet's trying to contact Earth, that's what I get. So I said that I didn't see what was so bloody funny and the Mad Cow told me to watch my language, as per usual. Sigmund's contribution, also as per usual, was to quote the only poem he knows—the one about seeing yourself as others see you. Too right, I said, and I removed myself from the kitchen in a meaningful way. I was **REALLY** irked. I mean, I listen to them all the time, not that any of them ever has much to say. (Yadda yadda yadda the government . . . yadda yadda yadda guess what happened in the supermarket . . . yadda yadda yadda . . . yadda yadda yadda . . . I mean, **BORING** or what?)

So that's why I decided it's definitely time to start the Dark Phase. Disha (*My v Best Friend in the Universe and Forever*) and I have been talking about it since September. I **REALLY** don't want to end up having a trivial life like everyone else, especially everyone I'm related to. I want to **LIVE**, not just exist. I mean, life isn't about what's on telly or who left the toilet seat up, is it? It's full of **ANGST** (meaning suffering and deep emotions) and **PASSION**. I want to be in touch with the **REAL** stuff. The **DEEP** pain and joy. The **TRUE** Essence and Substance. I have a *Questing, Artistic Soul,* and if I don't get away from all this mundane crap, it will wither and die like a flower in a desert.

4 Anyway, I was lying on my bed thinking about all of this when I remembered this diary. Sappho (aka my aunt Hannah) gave it to me as a winter solstice present. (Sappho doesn't give presents for Christmas because it's a Male, Capitalist, Consumer Bloodbath; she gives winter solstice presents instead.) It's called *The Lives of the Great Feminists Diary,* and it's packed with facts you never wanted to know about women you've never heard of. For instance, Fusae Ichikawa founded the Women's Suffrage League of Japan in 1924! I was **REALLY** glad to learn that! At last my life has meaning! Anyway, I was going to wait a couple of months and then throw it out without the Mad Cow noticing, which is what I usually do with presents from Sappho, but now I've changed my mind. Instead of trying to converse with people who don't want to listen, I'm going to seek solace and self-expression in the written word. I reckon that way I can get in touch with my **DEEPER SELF**. And also it should help my chances of finally getting a story published in the school magazine.

Rang Disha after the kitchen was finally evacuated by the peasants. She was suitably shocked by their behavior, though not, of course, surprised (she's known me a long time and knows what my family's like almost as well as I do). D says she reckons the Mad Cow squints like that when she's really trying to focus on something, though I can't imagine why she'd want to focus on Sigmund. I asked D where she gets this stuff from and she said from books. D's ready for the Dark Phase too.

I was going to tell you what happened at lunch, but I'm so emotionally depleted now that I can't exactly remember what it was.

FRIDAY 22 DECEMBER

Last day of school before the Christmas break, so it was v intensely busy. On top of everything else, I had to race to the shop during lunch because I left all my Christmas cards at home (the Mad Cow was nagging me this morning, as per usual, so I totally forgot about them). I got fifteen cards (including one from Ms. Staples, my English teacher and a constant source of inspiration to me), and a present from Siranee, who's going up north for the holidays.

Went round to Disha's after school to discuss the Dark Phase. Disha agrees that since we both turn seventeen next year (D's Libra and I'm Scorpio), it's an excruciatingly important time for us and if we're ever going to **REALLY LIVE** and not just go through the motions like our parents, we'd better start preparing for it now. Also we're both very ***Creative and Artistic***, and it's the Great Artists and Writers who have always known how to suffer. If they're not killing themselves or hacking off body parts, then they're full of **doom and gloom** and muttering about how awful everything is (Disha says she reckons Shakespeare was always in a Dark Phase). We owe it to ourselves to explore the Deep End of the Pool of Life. D and I decided the Dark Phase will begin on the **Stroke of Midnight** on New Year's Eve. We're going to be intense, serious, intellectually and spiritually curious and adventurous, and spend a lot of time nurturing our ***Souls***. To do this we're going to read poetry and great literature, really get into art and serious films, and wear mainly black clothes and makeup so everyone will know how deeply we experience things, etc. I'm v glad I changed my mind about chucking this diary. The Dark Phase and all its revelations, understandings, and epiphanies **MUST** be recorded!!!

The Mad Cow and Sigmund were arguing again at supper. (If things go on like this much longer, I'm going to demand combat pay.) The MC was all wound up because when Sigmund said he'd take her Christmas shopping tonight she didn't think he was going to bring along half of the single parents group he runs as well (this, of course, was a GROSS exaggeration on the MC's part; it was only Mrs. Kennedy). Anyway, when they broke for air, I took the opportunity to make my announcement re the Dark Phase. It really is the season of miracles, because for once (to my utter amazement) they were all listening. Sigmund said, "Does this mean you're leaving Earth's orbit for good?" The Mad Cow said I could forget getting any money from HER for a new wardrobe (as if!), and Justin, keeping to his policy of being as difficult and bloody-minded as possible, said that it wasn't the Great Artists and Writers who understood suffering; it was the poor sods nobody'd ever heard of. CAN YOU BELIEVE IT? My brother the philistine Neanderthal. Justin said that if I wanted to get in touch with the deepest levels of human angst I should try living on the streets! I didn't even stay for pudding after that. I went straight to my room. Obviously I'm starting the Dark Phase not a moment too soon!!!

SATURDAY 23 DECEMBER

Disha and I did some last-minute Christmas shopping today. (Except for D, I'm giving everyone either v cool candles or v cool picture frames that I got in the market.) We ran into David and Marcus. David wanted us to help him find something for his sister. This proved a little difficult. She doesn't read, she doesn't have any hobbies, she never writes letters, she has no interest in plants, and EVERYBODY always gets her bath oils, etc. (I ask you—what choice do they have?!!) On the basis that, if nothing else, David's sister must eat, Disha suggested food, but that was also out since David's sister's always on a diet. I finally cracked it and he got her a gift voucher at the video shop. (David thinks I may be a genius, but modesty made me point out that I am related to a psychotherapist.) To celebrate, we all went for lunch at this v cool Japanese noodle place. I was going to get another little present for the Mad Cow because Disha remembered that I gave her a candle for her birthday, but I spent more than I'd meant to on lunch. So we went for coffee instead. (Marcus and David, being male, don't really like shopping anyway. They find it v stressful and largely boring. D and I discussed it later and we agree that it's something to think about. I mean, they can play the same computer games for HOURS ON END, which we find EXCRUCIATINGLY TEDIOUS, yet when it comes to something that's actually quite intellectually demanding and stimulating they either get pissed off or fall asleep. Disha reckons it must be genetic.)

The Mad Cow dragged the Christmas tree in from the garden this afternoon, complaining the whole time like it was as big as the one at Buckingham Palace or something. (Defying all natural laws, it's exactly the same size it was last year, which isn't exactly enormous.) Sigmund's meant to do the lights, but he wasn't home so I got stuck with the job. Of course, the MC nagged me to check them before I put them on. None of them worked, but I put them on anyway. I don't have HOURS to waste testing every bloody bulb. Alice Bestler's having a bunch of us over to watch Christmas videos tonight.

* * *

LATER

Had a v good time at Alice's (her parents were smashed, so we helped ourselves to the eggnog), but came home to find the MC still up. Redecorating the Christmas tree. She was even grumpier than usual because she'd had to rush out to Woolworth's to get another set of lights. I told her the lights were working fine when I tested them, and she believed me. She's really not that bright.

SUNDAY 24 DECEMBER — CHRISTMAS EVE

When I was little, Christmas Eve was *Magical*. I'd wake up practically tingling with excitement. (One time I even threw up all over the kitchen table, I was so jazzed!) I'd lie awake for hours, listening for sleigh bells and singing angels and stuff like that. Oh, youth! How brief it is, and how deluded! (I know I'm only sixteen, but I already get a bittersweet feeling when I think about my childhood.) Now Christmas Eve is about as exciting as Groundhog Day (but with presents). The same people. The same food. The same arguments. To show you what I mean, Nan arrived this afternoon just in time for lunch (as per usual). The first thing Nan says *every year* is, "Doesn't the tree look beautiful?" And then she starts complaining about the ride over or her arthritis, etc. I said hello to Nan, and then I said I had to deliver my Xmas presents to my friends and got out of there **FAST** before Nan started banging on about God. When I got back, my mate David was waiting for me. The MC was force-feeding him her home-baked biscuits (which are more like pressed sand than what you buy) and Nan was going on about Why We Celebrate Christmas as though he'd never heard the story before. David was trying to smile and act interested and hungry and all, but I could tell that he was **V GLAD** to see me. There was definitely sweat on his forehead, which was excruciatingly attractive in a v virile way. I sort of go in and out of fancying David, but right then I was absolutely more in than out. In fact, I really wished it were snowing, because then we could have gone for a walk in a winter wonderland and had a snowball fight, which I know from films is a *v Romantic* thing to do. (And also v Christmassy, of course.) But since it wasn't even raining we went to my room.

David and I had a v interesting conversation about the hypocrisy of adults. Do what I say, but not what I do. Yadda yadda yadda, God and Peace on Earth and Goodwill to Men, but it's really all about selling as much crap as possible, and then the prime minister even tells everybody not to give anything to street beggars. What's that supposed to mean? I'm not on the God Squad or anything, but even I know that Jesus was v into helping beggars and people like that. I said maybe Nan should go round and read the PM the New Testament, because he seems to have missed a couple of crucial chapters. David agreed. David's pretty intelligent. He says his family behave even worse at Christmas than they do the rest of the year too. And they never give him what he wants. I said I was thinking of painting my room, and David said he'd help. (Even if I fancied doing the whole thing all by myself, I would've accepted—think how sweaty he'll get painting!!!) Then we exchanged our presents. I bet he got me something from the Body Shop. Even though he wrapped it himself to throw me, you can tell from the shape. And, anyway, boys aren't exactly imaginative shoppers, are they? David guessed I gave him a photo frame. He said he hoped there was a picture of me in it. What a brilliant idea! I wish I'd thought of it *before* I wrapped all my presents.

CHRISTMAS DAY

It was just us today. Sigmund, the Mad Cow, their other—
less successful—progeny, and Nan. Which was even more
dire than it sounds. The only bright spot was that Nan and
the MC *loved* their candles (I guess she forgot what I gave
her for her birthday—that's gratitude for you!), though
this was more than made up for by the fact that Sigmund
and Justin acted like I'd given them something secondhand.
By lunchtime Nan was well into God mode and the parents
were well into the Xmas booze.

There was a major row. Even worse than last year.
Sigmund's under orders not to argue with Nan at
Christmas because it's her favorite day next to Easter, but
how long he holds to that depends on how much he's had
to drink. Today he lasted till it was time to say grace. (Nan
always has to say grace, even when it isn't Xmas. Even at
breakfast, for God's sake!) For the first time since I've
known him, Sigmund volunteered for the job. The Mad
Cow gave him one of her Death by Laser Looks, but Nan
was delighted. (You'd think she'd know better; he's been
her son for more than half a century!) Sigmund closed his

eyes and bowed his head, all solemnlike, and then he started thanking God for the millions of people in the world who suffer hunger, poverty, oppression, torture, injustice, etc. "We're all very grateful that it isn't us," said Sigmund. "Very, very grateful." Justin (who has less of a sense of humor than he has brains if you ask me) thought it was hilarious, but neither Nan nor the Mad Cow so much as cracked a smile. Nan said there was a lot of evil in the world, and it had nothing to do with God, and Sigmund said how did you get to be the Supreme Creator and not have anything to do with evil? Nan said man had a **weak and wicked** side, and Sigmund wanted to know whose fault that was. Sigmund said that if God *had* created man, then He'd made a pretty big mess of it, hadn't He? But Nan's not one of those meek Christians. She started snapping and bristling and reminding Sigmund how long she was in labor with him (two weeks, apparently). Sigmund took his plate and a bottle of wine into his office (or the Bunker, as the MC's started calling it, because he spends so much time there lately). He stayed there for the rest of the afternoon, which didn't exactly kill the party. At least we got to finish eating in *Peace*. Sappho came round after we'd eaten because she's a vegan as well as a pagan and she won't sit in the same room as a turkey unless it's alive and extremely well.

Here's what I got for Christmas:

(1) **A MOBE**! This is the best present I ever got in my **ENTIRE** life! Especially since it came from Sigmund. Last year he gave me a gift voucher for Marks & Spencer (how tacky is that? He said I could use it to **BUY UNDERWEAR**—as if!!!) and this book called *Freud for Beginners*, which I dumped in the book bank. Sappho said giving a teenager a mobile phone was the equivalent of giving her a spear or a bow and arrow in more primitive cultures. Everyone laughed like she was making a joke, but I think she has a point. Must discuss with D.

(2) Besides the mobe, I got a phone card for fifty quid's worth of calls! That should last me **EONS**.

(3) A well wicked pair of knee-high black leather boots with the most incredible heels that the Mad Cow only got me because she said she wouldn't have any peace if she didn't. (I really had to turn the screws for this, believe me. I even had to **GO** with her to get them, because I knew she'd never buy them for me if I wasn't there to goad her on. I had enough trouble just getting her into the shop!)

(4) A T-shirt that says JESUS LOVES YOU from Nan (all four of us got the same thing). It's a slight improvement on last year when we all got pocket Bibles, but mine was in Korean.

(5) A book on yoga from Justin. I'm not exactly paralyzed

with joy by this one. Either Sigmund put him up to it, or Justin thinks it's funny to torture and torment me like this. What I really wanted was money for a class. Ms. Staples goes to one at the yoga center, which she says is v cool. I even bought this v wicked neon-purple leotard and matching leggings in case there were any deeply spiritual but excruciatingly attractive blokes about, but Sigmund refused to pay for the course. He said my piano, swimming, computer, and pottery lessons cost him **THOUSANDS,** and all he has to show for it is a piano nobody ever plays, an antique computer no one uses, and a bowl with a round bottom that he keeps his paper clips in. (6) Two lots of bath stuff from the Body Shop. (One from Marcus and one from David. They must have asked Disha what aroma I like because they're both Raspberry Ripple. This could be a problem, because Raspberry Ripple doesn't exactly fit with the Dark Phase. White Musk would be better.)

What I didn't get was an electric razor. God knows I dropped enough hints. And I practically **BLEED TO DEATH** every time I shave my legs. But I suppose I should've known I had as much chance of getting an electric razor as I had of getting a car. Even though Sigmund throws a **MEGA** wobbly every time I borrow his razor, and is

ALWAYS championing women and blathering on about what a feminist he is because sometimes he washes the dishes and stuff like that, he isn't v interested in female things. (I once asked him to get me some pads while he was in the chemist's and he practically went into cardiac arrest!) And I get no sympathy for that sort of thing from the MC either. Not only is she related to Sappho (who has hair under her ARMS!!!), but she's so far beyond being a sexual object that she's pretty much into the chimp look herself.

Oh, yes, and I also got (7) this excruciatingly cool top from Disha (it's black with the outline of a bat in purple glitter—V DARK!).

TUESDAY 26 DECEMBER — BOXING DAY

Disha had to go to her aunt's for dinner and her father made her leave her mobe at home. (D says getting a mobe isn't exactly the modern equivalent of getting your own spear because nobody was going to take your spear away from you because you used it too much, were they?) Anyway, since I'm stuck all alone in the House of

Horror I reckon this is a good time to put you in the picture re ME!

VITAL INFORMATION ABOUT ME:
Name: Janet Foley Bandry.
Age: Sixteen years and almost two months.
What I'm Like: I'm outgoing, but I can be quiet and v thoughtful—I don't consider myself superficial at all. I like to think about life and all the BIG questions a lot. Everybody says I have a wicked sense of humor. (I believe laughter is v important. I mean, what do you have if you don't have laughter? You have tears.) I'm interested in EVERYTHING, except things that are BORING. I'm pretty sure I'm heterosexual, even though there's lesbianism in the family and Sigmund's cousin Bryan is married to a bloke named Ethan. But I'm not just a thinker. I'm an action person too and I am planning a life that is full of *Romance and Adventure*.
Parents: Jocelyn Bandry, aka the Mad Cow, forty-five if she's a day, teacher (it's just like they say: those who can't do anything, teach); and Robert Bandry, aka Sigmund, fifty-five, some sort of psychotherapist.
Siblings: Justin Bandry, eighteen, dweeble and general cosmic fungus.
Favorite Colors: They used to be red and blue when I

was younger, but now that I'm more mature and about to embark upon my Dark Phase they're **black and purple**.

Favorite Foods:

(1) Hamburgers with lots of stuff on them.

(2) Roast beef and Yorkshire pudding.

(3) Chips (esp. with gravy).

(4) Fried chicken.

(5) Smoked salmon with cream cheese. I've only had this once, at Disha's, because it's too excruciatingly sophisticated for my family (who think a shred of paper towel is a serviette), but I really loved it (proving yet again that I was meant for greater things!).

Favorite Subjects in School: English and art.

Favorite Things in the Universe:

(1) *My Best Friend*, Disha Paski.

(2) Books.

(3) Films.

(4) Music.

(5) Hanging out with my mates.

(6) Exploring other dimensions and stuff like that.

(7) **LIFE**!!!

(8) Cats. It's no mystery why the Egyptians worshiped them, is it? They're not soppy and weak like dogs, but strong and v independent, qualities I definitely admire. (Other things I really like are rainy nights, the moon, plain

Bounty bars, tortilla chips, triple chocolate mousse, really big jumpers, silk, cold sheets, watching telly in the dark, pigs, etc.)

Most Hated Things in the Universe:

(1) PE and the Anti-Barbie (Mrs. "Don't Get Your Knickers in a Twist" Wist, my PE teacher).

(2) Science.

(3) Maths.

(4) Anything boring.

(5) Catriona Hendley.

(6) Cruelty and injustice.

Life Ambition: I'm not sure yet. I reckon I can work that out once I'm at university—if I go. I may go to art school instead, even though Justin goes to art school, which is hardly a recommendation. (Personally I think calling what Justin does art is pushing it. I mean, anybody can take a photo. We've got ALBUMS full of the bloody things, to prove my point. People don't queue for hours to see the *Mona Lisa* because da Vinci had a good camera, do they?) But I, of course, do not merely take photos; I'm a painter, so art's still a v definite possibility. On the other hand, literature is also a possibility. (I lean more towards literature because there are quite a few Great Women Writers but all the Great Artists are men. I don't see much point in entering a field with such limited potential.) On the other hand, maybe I'll travel and find myself in India or Australia or someplace like that instead, which is something both artists and writers often do.

Some Things That Really Annoy Me:

(1) My family.

(2) Women with pushchairs (you can't move without tripping over one).

(3) Pop music.

(4) People who pick their noses on the bus, etc.

(5) People who talk to themselves out loud in public.

(6) People who never listen to what other people are saying (esp. if the people not being listened to are in their teens).

(7) Catriona Hendley.

That's not absolutely everything, and I do change my mind (which is, of course, a sign of personal growth as well as a *Creative Nature*), but it gives you a rough idea.

WEDNESDAY 27 DECEMBER

Two whole days of family festivities is about all I can bear without applying for citizenship in another country, so since Disha was dragged to Kent to see some old gene sharer, I sought refuge at Sara Dancer's. Sara Dancer lives with her dad because she had this **GINORMOUS** fight with her mother in the summer, and her mother said that if she hated it so much living with her she should go and live with her father. Sara says her father's not exactly **COOL** (he's an accountant) but it's a lot less stressful living with him than with her mother because he doesn't give a toss if there are dishes in the sink, etc. Sara says the difference between living with a male parent and a female parent is like the difference between buying your groceries in a superstore and in the corner shop. Sara Dancer says she thinks she may **DO IT** soon. She says she can't stop thinking about sex, so why not? I said because she never has more than two dates with the same boy, and she agrees that this is her **MAJOR** stumbling block. And also she reckons that though it would be easy to do it with the Johnny Depp of *Sleepy Hollow*, and maybe with Russell Crowe, she's not so sure about anyone she actually knows. Which is probably just as well since Sara's mother would kill her if Sara did it and she found out.

Talked to D on my mobe after she got home from her mission of mercy, which was (surprise, surprise) incredibly boring. (D says she doesn't know how **ANYONE** could live anywhere but London but I pointed out that true *Creative Spirits* can draw inspiration from anywhere. Look at van Gogh—he was always doing flowers.) Wound up having a v intense conversation. D says it's no wonder that Sara can't stop thinking about **SEX** since it's always being pushed in your face. Songs about sex, ads using sex, films about sex. It just goes on and on . . . Disha says she reckons if everybody had good sex (or even bad sex) on a regular basis they wouldn't need to talk about it all the time. I asked D if she thinks it's man's nature to deceive himself, and she says Shakespeare's always banging on about that. D says I'm definitely going to be a natural at the Dark Phase.

I think I must have what Sigmund calls "a low libido" (apparently another thing I can thank the Mad Cow for), because I'm not sex mad at all. What I think about a lot more than sex is *Falling in Love*. I want it to be like Romeo and Juliet or Jane Eyre and Mr. Rochester. I want to be swept away by *Passion,* a hopeless fool for *Love*! (Not like Sappho's friend Samantha, who seems to get swept away every time some bloke buys her dinner.) Disha agrees with me about love and passion, of course, but she says she's afraid we may have a long wait before we find men who inspire those feelings. She says look at the boys at school—most of them couldn't inspire a drop of water from a rain cloud. I said not even David or Marcus? Disha says she likes them both as people, and she does see that each in his way is more attractive than most of them, but she once saw Marcus run a piece of dental floss from one nostril to the other, which pretty much deleted passion from that menu. And she's not **TOTALLY** sure about David, but at least he doesn't wear trainers, which is so *très passé*. (I mean, really, the parents both own a pair!)

THURSDAY 28 DECEMBER

24

Went to get the paint for my room today. Disha couldn't come because her mother was pissed off about something and made her stay in to help her with the housework. (At least that's one thing the MC wouldn't even *consider*! She learned her lesson the time she made me do the vacuuming and the Hoover caught fire.) There was this **V OBNOXIOUS** man on the bus who told me off because I was talking to Disha on my mobe. I couldn't believe it! He said I should get a life instead of spending my parents' hard-earned money telling my friends I was on a bus. I told him I already had a **LIFE,** and it included being part of the age of communication, and that he was the one who should get a life instead of butting in on someone's private conversation. People are **TOO MUCH!** Really. It's no wonder the sensitive suffer.

Stopped at the bookshop on the way home. I reckoned this would be a good time to read one of the books Ms. Staples is always talking about. Deep, meaningful, angst-filled modern classics are her speciality. I got *The Outsider* by Albert Camus because Ms. Staples says he was into the absurdity of life, and because I definitely identify with the title (the *Spiritually and Creatively Gifted* are always on the outside, aren't they?). And also because it was about three thousand pages shorter than *Ulysses* (another of Ms. Staples's favorites).

FRIDAY 29 DECEMBER

I'm absolutely exhausted! Marcus and David came round to help me and Disha paint my room today. I could only find two rollers, so Disha and I did the woodwork with brushes. It looks well wicked! We did the walls purple and the woodwork black. It's v sophisticated, but powerful and moody at the same time. You can imagine someone sitting in it, writing poetry and listening to jazz. (Which, of course, is what I plan to do!)

My family has the aesthetics of wildebeests—which probably isn't v fair to wildebeests. Not one of them appreciates the new decor of my room. The Mad Cow said it reminded her of a whorehouse. I asked her if she was saying this from previous experience, or if she was just basing it on her wide knowledge of whorehouses in general, and she told me I wasn't half as funny as I thought I was (how original is that?!!). Nan said that she would never have been allowed to get away with painting her room like that When She Was a Girl. I said I was surprised she could remember that far back.

26

Started *The Outsider*. The narrator's mother dies on page one, which seems promising. I fell asleep though before I could get any further. Thank God I didn't get *Ulysses*, or I'd be reading it for the rest of my life!!!

MONDAY 1 JANUARY

A NEW YEAR BEGINS!
WE EMBRACE LIFE ANEW!

D and I were invited to a Bruce Lee Festival at Marcus's for New Year's Eve but we declined. Even though I find boys can be pretty interesting on their own, when you get a few of them together their maturity level collapses in a v alarming way. They think a car chase is intellectually challenging. Disha agrees. She says it sometimes strikes her as Absolutely Amazing that all of the Great Thinkers are men. It doesn't really seem possible.

So since Disha's parents went out last night, D and I spent a quiet New Year's Eve at hers. In anticipation of this momentous upcoming year, we both wore black jeans and tops, and black lipstick and eye shadow. The effect was excruciatingly DP. There was a bottle of white wine in the fridge, and Disha said we could take it because her parents had had so much to drink over the last week they wouldn't notice. I'd nicked a couple of fags from Sigmund's **LAST** pack (this time he says he really is giving up for good). We don't smoke, of course (never mind the heart disease, etc., have you **SEEN** what nicotine does to your **TEETH**?), but we reckoned it was a special occasion so we should try it the once. (And also **MASSES** of Great Artists and Writers have been addicted to tobacco as well as alcohol, so we reckoned it was fitting for the beginning of the Dark Phase.) Disha managed a whole one, but I was coughing too much to exactly enjoy it, and it made me feel sick to my stomach. But the wine was great. (If I have to be addicted to something because of my *Creative Spirit,* I would definitely prefer white wine to something that could give you cancer and ruin your smile. Plus Sappho says

white wine's **NOT FATTENING,** and everything else
I like is!!! We lit a bunch of candles and some incense,
found a jazz program on the radio, and sat on the floor of
Disha's room. We talked for **HOURS**. Mainly about life.
It was all v deep and intense, and v intellectual. Disha said
it was too bad the wine wasn't one of those bottles in a
straw basket, since that was much more Dark Phase than
chardonnay, but I said wine was the drink of intellectuals
no matter what it was in. D puked in her waste bin in the
middle of the night, but the wine must've knocked me out
because I didn't hear her. Neither of us even had a
headache today. But Disha told her mum she thought she
had a touch of flu, so she didn't even have to clean out the
waste bin herself.

I don't believe in making New Year's resolutions. I believe
in constant and continuous personal growth. My parents,
being *très* mundane, make resolutions every year—and
usually break them by noon on January first. So, this isn't
a resolution, but one thing I am going to do this year
is listen to more jazz. Disha and I really enjoyed the
program on the radio last night, even though a lot
of the time there wasn't any tune you could actually
recognize. But that's because jazz is the music of the
intellectual, so it's meant to be like that. In our house
all that's usually played is the music of the bourgeois

(Sigmund's Capital Gold and the MC's classical tapes) and the depraved (the noise Justin listens to). And also I'm going on a diet. It's not like I'm **OBESE** or anything, but artists, writers, and intellectuals in a Dark Phase tend to be lean. (Disha said that's because they're usually too poor to eat, but I pointed out that the artist who sold her bed to the Saatchi Gallery isn't poor, and Disha said that just because someone put your bed in a gallery didn't make you Rembrandt, who anyway was **FAT**. I hope she's not going to spend the Dark Phase being argumentative.)

When I got back to the House of Horror, the MC and Sigmund had had another **MAJOR ROW**. I knew as soon as I got into the flat because the MC was muttering darkly on the phone to Sappho. Sigmund only emerged from the Bunker for supper, and they didn't say a word to each other for the whole meal. Personally I prefer it when they're not speaking since at least it's quiet.

TUESDAY 2 JANUARY

Life really is v ironic, isn't it? (This is something I've been noticing more and more lately.) Every morning during term I drag myself out of bed and listen to the news hoping that a small fire's closed my school for at least one day, but when it's the holidays I'm **BORED OUT OF MY MIND**!!! Disha, of course, feels exactly the same. She says she's finding the holiday stultifying (meaning it's turning her brain into oatmeal). I asked her where she got that word from, and she said that just shows how bad it is, doesn't it? She's started reading the dictionary for fun. Thank God Marcus rang up and said everybody was hanging out at David's this afternoon if we'd like to come along. Do birds like to fly? Not only were we **DYING** to get out of the house, but this was our Dark Phase debut, so to speak. (Disha got a red leather jacket for Xmas, which is unfortunate since even though it's cooler than ice it **RUINS** the effect. Thank God my boots are black.) The Mad Cow wanted to know if I was going to a funeral (is that funny, or what?!!), and Sigmund said no, it was just the way creatures on my planet dress (surely I must've been adopted!). It took me and D so long to get totally ready that by the time we got to David's, Marcus had already gone home! After inviting us and everything. It's too much, really.

Except for David (who said we looked **v Morticia Addams**), none of the others even noticed our new look! They were too busy stuffing their faces and playing the PlayStation game David got for Xmas, which was **V BORING,** esp. if you were practically starving to death. It made me think about the power of telly and stuff like that. Their reality's totally distorted. You should've heard them banging on about tactics like they were crack SAS troops and not teenage boys who can't get across London without an A–Z. My feet were hurting a bit from my new boots and my stomach was starting to growl (all I'd had all day was ONE slice of DRY toast and two v small apples) and D looked like she might fall asleep, so we decided to leave. Fortunately I've had new boots before, so I'd thought to bring a pair of shoes with me. I changed as soon as we got out of the house and was able to walk home without doing my feet any permanent damage, even though I didn't look as cool. I was RAVENOUS by the time I got home, of course. I stood at the counter and ate half a packet of water biscuits, which I reckon is OK since they don't have any fat in them. Not so sure about the cheese.

WEDNESDAY 3 JANUARY

I think the Mad Cow's really starting to lose it (she is pushing fifty). If she's not picking fights with Sigmund, she's picking them with me! I sat down to have a cup of tea with her this afternoon while she was cooking something, and she went **BERSERK** because I sniffed the milk. I just wanted to make sure it hadn't gone off. Is that a crime? I swear that I am not going to become grumpy and senile when I get old. I'm going to have a *Young Heart and Soul,* even when I'm sixty. And maybe plastic surgery.

D says it sounds to her like the MC must be **MENOPAUSAL**!!! She says she's heard of cases where the woman either won't come out of her room for months or does weird things like painting the entire flat bright orange (sometimes on the **OUTSIDE**!!!). When her nan went through the menopause she thought that ghosts were after her and kept climbing into the washing machine because she thought she'd be safe there (it was a top loader).

THURSDAY 4 JANUARY

Went with Disha to exchange my two gift sets of Raspberry Ripple for two sets of White Musk, but the sales assistant wouldn't exchange them because I didn't have the receipts. I asked her where else she thought they came from, since they say Body Shop on them, but she was a right stubborn cow. Disha says I can always use them as presents for other people, as long as I don't give her one.

The Mad Cow was sitting in the kitchen, sniffing into a cup of tea, when Disha and I got back. I couldn't tell whether or not she'd been crying, but she looked like she was getting into one of her **Moods**. We made ourselves scarce. Disha says the MC seems **V TENSE** lately, but I explained that it's just her hormones. She's up and down like a staircase. You never know what mood she's going to be in. D says she hopes that if we ever get that old they'll have invented some drugs to combat it.

FRIDAY 5 JANUARY

Andrew "the Missing Link" Jeffers, Justin's best mate for reasons that will become obvious, accosted me in the kitchen while I was making myself a cup of tea. He wanted me to know that he thinks my friend Disha is v fit. I said that's because she works out and has a black belt in karate, and he said that wasn't what he meant. (Really? Um, duh. . . ! I didn't know that!) He said to tell her she has great tits. I told him to tell her himself.

SATURDAY 6 JANUARY

According to The Lives of the Great Feminists, Virginia Woolf is
famous for saying that every woman should have a room
of her own. You can tell right off that she didn't live with
my family. I woke up this morning to find the child my
parents should **NEVER** have had standing over my bed
taking pictures of me! (I wouldn't sleep in the nude in this
house in a heat wave.) It's all the Mad Cow's fault for
getting him that new camera for Christmas. (She's always
spoiled him!) Now he's started taking pictures of US again.
Of course, the MC's on his side, as per usual. She says
Justin doesn't mean any harm; he's just obsessed.
Possessed, more like. Then she went off on one of her
tangents, yammering on about how talented Justin is and
how proud she is of him. (For pushing a button!) The MC
says that Justin wants to experiment more with style, now
that he's made a bit of a name for himself. I said and what
would that name be? Shithead? She thought I was joking.
Personally I think she's delusional. (I can only assume that
my father the shrink hasn't noticed this because he's not
home or they're fighting or he's in the Bunker pretending
to be working but really sneaking fags.) It was soooo

excruciatingly **BORING**. I was tempted to tell her that Justin takes pictures of her and Sigmund sleeping as well, but I decided to use the information to blackmail him instead. I need the money.

Talked to Disha for **EONS** last night. It's so civilized, being able to lie on my bed in privacy and have a conversation without everybody eavesdropping on my business or constantly interrupting to tell me the time or that they're waiting for a call. I'm going to need another phone card soon.

SUNDAY 7 JANUARY

Disha and I hung out with the others at David's again this afternoon, and this time Marcus managed to stay for more than two seconds. Marcus suggested we go for a walk and then David said he'd come too. Marcus got us laughing so much I had to go into a pub to use the loo. I pretended I was looking for my mother. After Marcus and David went home, Disha and I went back to mine. Justin and Andrew were in the kitchen. I went to the loo and Justin went off to get something and can you believe it? The Missing Link **DID IT**! He actually **DID IT**! He told Disha she had great

tits! And then he tried to **TOUCH THEM**! I lied about
Disha being a black belt, but she did take a self-defense
course from the police last summer because her parents
are refugees. She flipped Andrew over and he crashed into
the fridge. Disha and I didn't stop laughing for **HOURS**.
I got yelled at by the MC for knocking most of the
magnets off the fridge, of course. Like it was **MY** fault,
right? And then she made **ME** pick them up, not Justin!
Talk about **INEQUALITY** between the sexes! I should
ask Sappho who I should complain to.

MONDAY 8 JANUARY

What an excruciating relief to get back to the real world
after all that time imprisoned in the **House of Horror**! And
also, of course, I was glad to see my many friends and Ms.
Staples (my English and **FAVORITE** teacher). There was
a lot to catch up on! Catriona Hendley spent most of the
day boring everyone with tales of her excruciatingly
wonderful holiday in **NEW YORK** (of course! Where
else would she go; they're not selling tickets to Mars yet,
are they?), and all the famous people she met, and all the
amazing restaurants she ate in, and all the astounding
things she did (like shopping till—cue hysterical laughter

here—she couldn't shop anymore!!!). Step aside, Columbus. You'd think **SHE** discovered America, the way she went on. It was **TOTALLY** revolting. Not all was **gloom and doom,** however. Disha, Siranee, Alice, and I all noticed that Catriona had put on a few pounds eating in all those amazing restaurants. Her chest bones aren't protruding as much as usual. Unfortunately this also means that I'll **NEVER** be able to go to New York unless I lose at least a stone beforehand. And so far I apparently haven't lost a gram. I'm going to have to stop my diet until the MC buys a decent set of scales (i.e., ones that work). What's the point of starving if every time I weigh myself I'm heavier than I was the time before?

Wore my new boots to school for the first time today. **EVERYONE** admired them. Even Catriona Hendley said they were très cool and asked where I got them. Wiping a tear from my eye, I sadly had to tell her they were the last pair in the shop. Which is why they're a little tight (though I didn't tell her that, of course). I was starting to limp by the end of the day, but I don't think anyone noticed.

TUESDAY 9 JANUARY

I asked Mr. Belakis, my art teacher, why there aren't any Great Women Artists, and he said what about Frida Kahlo, to name but one. Then he told me to read some book by Germaine Greer. Found Germaine in my diary. Apparently there are **HORDES** of Great Women Artists, but no one ever tells you about them. Then I found Frida in my diary. Apparently she had one eyebrow, a mustache, and slept with **TONS** of people of **BOTH** sexes.

Had to soak my feet when I got home because of the blisters. Despite the pain I was in, the Mad Cow threw a **MAJOR** wobbly because I used the stew pot (it was the largest thing I could find). She said why didn't I use the mop bucket? I didn't know we had a mop bucket, but even if I had I wouldn't have put my feet in it. (After she's used it to wash the floors?) Disha says I can probably stretch them (the boots, not my feet).

I mentioned Frida Kahlo to Sappho, so she'll know I'm finally using something she gave me. Sappho said Frida's husband (who was also a famous artist) had a mustache and slept with **TONS** of people too, so what was the big deal?

WEDNESDAY 10 JANUARY

There really isn't any justice in this world, is there? The school magazine met this afternoon, and the next issue's going to have **TWO** poems by Catriona "God Died and Left Me in Charge" Hendley that she wrote about New York. One's called "Skyline" (how *très* original!) and the other's entitled "Invisible People" (about the poor—like she's ever met any). They're both really stupid poems if you ask me. Esp. the one about the invisible poor. All I can say is New York must be v different to London. Here poor people are right in your face. And you can't move down the street without tripping over their blankets and dogs, etc.

Meanwhile, **NOBODY** liked the story I submitted before Christmas. They found it confusing. But isn't life confusing? I talked to Ms. Staples about it in private. She had some v constructive things to say (*good imagery! nice use of language! gripping idea!*), but she says I need to work a bit harder on my plots. I told her I thought plots belonged in gardens, and that to conform to rigid rules about stuff like that stifled my *Creative Spirit*. Ms. Staples laughed and said that she hoped I didn't take that line when it came to my GCSEs because the education authority likes plots.

I could never be a teacher. It must suck the *Soul* right out of you (e.g., Jocelyn Bandry, though it is possible that she never had a soul in the first place). I feel bad for poor Ms. Staples, who, unlike my female parent, does have a *Passionate Soul* and a questing, intelligent mind despite the personal lack of talent that must've driven her into teaching. How depressing it must be to work for people who don't understand literature or art or the true nature of life! I told her I'd do my best. She gave me a grateful smile. It's a **BIG** responsibility, having to keep Ms. Staples's level of hope up, but I feel I'm old enough now to handle it. After all, that's part of what life's about, isn't it?

THURSDAY 11 JANUARY

What a day! I don't think any more could go wrong if I tried! The Mad Cow forgot to iron the gray skirt I was going to wear, so I had to find something else that fit my mood. It took **EONS**. I missed my usual bus, of course, and then I couldn't find my pass. I took *everything* out of my bag, but it wasn't *anywhere*. You should've heard the driver moan about how much stuff I carry around with me. (What's it to him? He's not my mother!) I asked him if he thought I was lugging around all these schoolbooks to get a free ride! I mean, really, if there was ever a man in **DESPERATE** need of a life, this was the man.

When I finally got to school, Disha turned up wearing almost the exact same shirt I was wearing, so we went back to hers so she could change. We were really only seconds late, but Stalin (aka Mr. Wilkins, our tutor) wouldn't listen to our perfectly reasonable explanation and gave us detention. (Power corrupts, and absolute power corrupts absolutely. I can't remember where I heard that, but it's true.) Then it turned out that besides forgetting to iron my skirt, the Mad Cow forgot to remind me to take my PE kit again. I told Mrs. Wist that I had cramps so bad I thought I was giving birth, and she let me go to the library instead of running around the field having my shins clubbed. The bad news was that the sight of me reminded the librarian, Mrs. Higgle, that I still had two books outstanding. I tried to explain that I thought I'd brought them back, but she said that was what I said last time. It'll be a note home next, and then Sigmund will get on my case, yadda yadda yadda. The man can talk you into unconsciousness. I hope the Mad Cow can find the books.

LATER

OH, TRAGEDY! OH, DARK DAY OF HORROR
AND GLOOM! I CAN'T FIND MY MOBE! And
I thought nothing more could go **WRONG** today! How
ironic is that? Why does everything happen to **ME**?
I must've dropped it on the bus this morning, which
is understandable considering all the trauma I was put
through! The last time I remember having it was when
I rang Sara Dancer at the bus stop. The parents will
dehydrate me if they find out.

FRIDAY 12 JANUARY

I'm meant to be tidying my room. ("If you want to go to
Disha's tonight, you'd better tidy that room!" I don't know
why she doesn't put it on a tape loop and save herself the
trouble of saying the same thing **OVER AND OVER**.)
The good news is that I thought I heard her coming to
check on me (she was definitely a prison guard in one of
her previous lives), so I dived under my bed in cleaning
mode, and guess what I found? The yoga book I got for
Christmas! I'd forgotten all about it. The woman on the

cover is sitting cross-legged and smiling. There are dozens of quotes on the back from ordinary people who say that yoga changed their lives. It looks pretty easy. I can smile, and I can sit cross-legged, so what could be so hard? Maybe I'll give it a try. I can see yoga fitting in v well with the Dark Phase. Ms. Staples does yoga and she says it's *vSpiritual*, as well as healthy. I wonder if you can lose weight doing yoga (since dieting obviously doesn't work).

SATURDAY 13 JANUARY

Had a v good time at Disha's, as per usual. Her parents aren't as obtrusive as some. We were going to have an **Exploring Other Dimensions Night,** but I left the book on witchcraft at home and Disha couldn't find the tarot cards I gave her for Christmas (you've got to be given them; you can't buy them for yourself), so we decided to have an Intellectual Night instead. We were going to get out this brilliant Japanese film Ms. Staples told us about, but Blockbuster didn't have it. We were going to listen to intelligent music and read poetry instead, but we couldn't find the jazz station. All was **FRUSTRATION AND DOOM** until Disha remembered that Mrs. Foster next door (who is civilized and has cable) lent her a copy of *Clueless* last year that we never watched. Ms. Staples says *Clueless* is based on a Jane Austen novel, so we reckoned that was just as good as something in Japanese. We finally found it under some stuff on the floor of Disha's wardrobe. But then frustration and doom turned to **AMAZEMENT AND SHOCK!** Someone who was probably Mr. Foster taped over *Clueless* with an **ADULT MOVIE**. We're not naive—we've seen the magazines on the top shelf in the news agent's and stuff like that, of course—but both Disha and I come from homes where pornography is frowned upon. Even Sigmund and the MC, who are major believers in free speech, say it's demeaning to women. Sappho said if she ever found Justin with porn she'd make him eat it, and not even Justin would think that was an idle threat. As for the Paskis, they were both arrested for disorderly conduct when someone tried to open a sex shop in their old neighborhood. (Mrs. P whacked the store owner over the head with a sign that said CHILDREN LIVE HERE.) We didn't watch much (you don't have to watch much to get the idea, and after that it's sort of boring). Disha says now she'll never be able to see the Fosters (esp. Mr. Foster) without feeling embarrassed. We talked a bit about the boys we know and whether or not they're into porn, which is a bit weird and creepy to think about. Then Disha said could I imagine either of our mothers straddling a chair in black lace suspenders with tassles hanging from her nipples and her tongue out like that, and we practically died laughing.

When I got back to **Bleak House** this afternoon, the Mad Cow was lying in wait (and not in suspenders and tassles, believe me. She might be into S&M though. I have no trouble picturing her with a whip). I barely got the door shut before she started in. "What did I tell you. . . ? What did you promise. . . ? I thought you were going to clean up that pigsty before you went out last night!" Same old same old. Then she literally dragged me over to the sink so I could see all the plates and stuff she'd found under my bed. **AND** she actually made me count them: six glasses, seven mugs, two plates, nine spoons, three bowls, and Great-Grandmother Rose's **WILLOW PLATE**!!! (Was I **INSANE**? How could I treat a family heirloom like that?) I told her to chill out. "A woman your age shouldn't get so excited," I told her. "You'll give yourself a stroke." For a minute there I thought she was going to forget about her commitment to nonviolent parenting and give *me* a stroke, but instead she asked me to let her know when my planet was ready to receive transmissions from Earth so she wasn't just wasting her breath all the time. And then she told me to **GO AND TIDY** my room, and not to come down till it was done. I may spend the rest of my life up here. (At least I would if I had a phone!)

SUNDAY 14 JANUARY

Disha wanted to know if I managed to stretch my new boots. I groaned out loud! Disha'd said I should wet them before I stuffed them full of newspaper so they'd be more flexible when I stretched them, so on Wednesday I filled the mop bucket with water and left them in it in the garden shed. I **TOTALLY** forgot about them! Disha said when she told me to soak them, she meant for an hour or so, not nearly a **WEEK**. What a **DISASTER**!!! I must've been cursed at birth or something. They look all funny, and the heel came off the right boot. Disha said I could take it to a cobbler, but I was too depressed to ask her what a cobbler is.

I hate my brother more than anyone has ever hated **ANYONE** or **ANYTHING** in the history of the world. As if it wasn't enough that my new boots are **TOTALLY RUINED,** I was just trying out some new makeup

(**Sorceress Black**) when the door to my room was flung open
and there was Justin and his bloody camera (we at 73A
Wooster Crescent live in a virtually lockless world). He got
me putting on eyeliner. I really think it's time they had
him put down. You can't bite into a crisp in this house
without being photographed. It's like living with the
paparazzi (but without the champagne and stuff). Poor
Princess Di! I really feel for what she went through. Death
must've been a kind of release. (When I told that to Disha,
she said maybe it's not just the *Creative* who suffer—the
famous do too. I never thought of it like that. I mean,
you can be **MEGA FAMOUS** and have the *Soul*
of a cow pat, can't you? But D says one has to make
a distinction between physical suffering and spiritual
suffering. Spiritual suffering is what the creative do.
I don't think it's premature to say that the Dark Phase is
v successful so far!)

41

MONDAY 15 JANUARY

Sara Dancer says her mother's boyfriend is into porn,
which Sara says is pretty understandable, since her mother
isn't exactly Madonna (she looks like a dinner lady). Sara

even found magazines with names like *Sex Slaves* and *She's Gotta Have It* under the rug in the bathroom. She won't take baths anymore. Sara's mother doesn't know it, but Sara's little brother watches porn all the time on cable. And also on the Internet. Sara watched it there once, out of intellectual curiosity, and it was pretty gross. She says she's searched her dad's flat for signs of Solitary Sexual Activity but all she turned up was a packet of condoms, which she took as a good sign even though she doesn't think he has a steady girlfriend. Sara says there's no way she'd put up with a room without a lock in her mother's house—not even when she's just there for a visit. She says it's like living with wild lions. You never know when their primitive nature is going to take over and they attack. I said you don't think your mum's boyfriend would **DO SOMETHING,** do you, and she said no, of course not, but you can't be too careful, can you? Look at all the articles in the papers about people molesting minors. Maybe newspapers aren't as **BORING** as I've always thought. (And also reading papers might be good for stimulating the **Depression and Sense of Suffering** of the DP. At least they're faster to read than most of Ms. Staples's books!)

I don't see how I can go another day without a phone. It's like having a limb amputated. I can still feel it pressed against my cheek. I can still see the special purple case

I bought for it. I can still hear its distinctive call (some Beatles song). I reach out for it and it isn't there. My fingers touch the air and I wonder why. Why? Why has this happened to me? (I reckon I must be learning an important life lesson in loss—you know, that **NOTHING** lasts forever—but I still wish I could've lost something else. Like Justin, for instance.) D says maybe I should've checked lost property, but everybody knows that anything good that gets lost gets nicked, so why bother? Now I have nothing to do when I'm waiting for buses or walking down the street on my own. It's **SO BORING**! And also it's torture.

Since I can't just lie on my bed and talk to Disha, I was going to watch some telly to relax before I started my homework, but Nan turned up. I was just about to open the living-room door when I heard her say, "Ask yourself what Jesus would do in this situation, Jocelyn." God knows what they're on about now, but I should think it would be hard even for Jesus to be in the place of a menopausal madwoman. I beat a hasty retreat.

TUESDAY 16 JANUARY

THIS IS TOO MUCH!!! You want to know how **TOTALLY INSANE** the Mad Cow's getting? Now she's going through the rubbish. **REALLY!!!** I asked her if she's planning to become a bag lady when she finally retires from making my life hell, and she said she was actually thinking of joining MI5. She said she was looking for evidence of Sigmund still being a closet nicotine addict. You'd think she'd remember from last time that he always sneaks the rubbish from the Bunker into someone else's bin so we can't accidentally find his butts. Anyway, she went through the rubbish and she found the boots. She went **BALLISTIC**! I mean, they're only **BOOTS**. They can be replaced. If you ask me, she's way too materialistic. She should try nurturing her spiritual side a bit more.

WEDNESDAY 17 JANUARY

Sigmund was banging on about work, as per usual,
while the rest of us were trying to eat our supper. I wasn't
really listening (I mean, who *does?*), but I heard him say
something about matrophobia. I hate to ask Sigmund
questions (because he always gives such v long answers
that by the time he's finished you don't have a clue what
you actually asked in the first place), but the Dark Phase
is one of intellectual curiosity, so I risked it. Sigmund said
matrophobia is when you're afraid of turning into your
own mother. Justin spoke one of his first full sentences
of the new year then. He asked Sigmund what it would
be called if he was afraid of *Sigmund* turning into *Nan*.
Everybody laughed except me. I was practically turned
to stone. It never even occurred to me before that such
a thing could happen. I know I worry about becoming
as **shallow and pointless** as the rest of my family, but it
never occurred to me that I could actually turn into MY
MOTHER. I asked Sigmund if that sort of thing was very
common, and he said it was much more common to turn
into your own mother than to be afraid of it. I couldn't
believe it! Me, turn into the Mad Cow?!! I'd have to kill

myself! I mean, really, what other option would I have? Now I'm feeling 𝕯𝖊𝖊𝖕𝖑𝖞 𝕯𝖊𝖕𝖗𝖊𝖘𝖘𝖊𝖉. All the years they make you go to school to memorize a bunch of crap that you immediately forget, but nobody ever tells you anything **REALLY IMPORTANT**. It doesn't seem fair. Are we mushrooms that have to be kept in the dark?

D agrees that no one ever tells you anything **REALLY IMPORTANT** or even worth knowing. She says the more she finds out in the DP, the more she realizes that it's practically a miracle that **EVERYBODY** isn't depressed. **TOO TRUE!** It almost makes you admire people like my parents, who manage to exist on such a superficial level that the slings and arrows of Outrageous Fortune miss them entirely. But can you truly experience **REAL** joy or meaning by floating on the surface of the Lake of Life and never diving down to the depths? Disha and I don't think so.

THURSDAY 18 JANUARY

There is a God! There really is! And He's **ON MY SIDE**!!! Sigmund caught Justin getting ready to take a picture of him while he was peeing (Sigmund, not Justin) and he went **BERSERK**!!! You'd never believe Sigmund makes his living being reasonable in this dead calm way if you'd seen him waving the roll of film about. He would've had the camera too, but the Mad Cow snatched it away just in time. I think she thought it was funny, because she left the room v quickly after that. I thought it was hilarious. Sigmund got so worked up that he got one of his migraines and had to go to bed.

Thursday nights I usually mind Mrs. Kennedy's twins, Shane and Shaun, while she goes to her computer class and then out for a drink with her mates, but tonight she rang to say she had a cold and wasn't going out after all. Mrs. Kennedy is in several of Sigmund's groups (including the wives of men in prison support group and the low self-esteem group), and now, under the guidance of a man who can never find his car keys, she's getting her life together. At four quid an hour, she can get everyone's life together for all I care. Not that the twins are easy. But God knows I could use the money (getting money out of Sigmund or the Mad Cow is harder than putting your eye makeup on in the dark); I could also really use the break from them, though. Children definitely don't fit into the DP. From what I can tell, most of the Great Writers and Artists didn't have that much to do with children—if anything. Not even the women. D agrees. She says

Shakespeare had the twins and all, but she doesn't think he took them every other weekend or anything like that. On the other hand, the MC doesn't like Mrs. Kennedy, so me going over there usually winds her up (one has to snatch bits of happiness where one can in this life!). The MC says she doesn't like Mrs. Kennedy because she shows right-wing racist tendencies (she votes Tory and once asked the MC what her ethnic background is), but I reckon it's really because Mrs. Kennedy's v attractive in an *EastEnders* sort of way, and the MC (being about as attractive as bog roll) resents her. It's a pretty common syndrome.

FRIDAY 19 JANUARY

Disha and I had another long talk about **MEN AND LOVE** this afternoon. Should I go after David? Should I go after Marcus? It's a big decision to make. Marcus is a v good artist, which gives us a *Spiritual Connection,* but he's got a v square face and only one eyebrow and isn't as good-looking as David. David's v sexy (D and I agree it's his eyes—his lashes are longer than mine when I'm wearing lash-lengthening mascara), and though he isn't a painter, he is v literary. (One time when we were all at his and excruciatingly bored, we played his parents' Trivial

Pursuit and David was incredible! Even Disha was impressed, and you already know how much she reads!) But he did start a food fight at Lila Jenkins's Halloween party, which was v juvenile, even though he did get Catriona Hendley smack in the face with a handful of jelly, which was pretty hilarious and ruined her hair! Sometimes I think that if I could put David and Marcus together I'd have the perfect man. After all, if you do end up having sex with someone, you get to be on pretty intimate terms with his penis, don't you? I don't think I'd be able to be on intimate terms with the penis of someone less than close to perfect. And also I do worry that there's no real *Frisson,* as the French (who seem to know a lot about *Passion and Romance*) would say. There's no real chemistry, no explosion of *Souls*. On the other hand, a little practice might not hurt. Maybe passion's something you have to work up to. As Disha says, you don't jump into the deep end of the pool the first time you try to swim, do you?

SATURDAY 20 JANUARY

GOD LOVES ME! He really does. Or maybe my karma's better than I thought, because wait till you hear what happened tonight. My whole family evacuated the premises after supper. Together! I think they were going to some exhibition at Justin's college. The parents were pretty presentable looking, but Justin is **NEVER** presentable looking; he always looks like he lives on the streets. The Mad Cow asked me if I was coming and I sighed and told her I had too much homework this weekend (which is pretty much true). Having the flat to myself is about as rare as seeing a flock of pigs flying over north London, so I decided to take advantage of this unexpected opportunity and as soon as they left I had a look for the Mad Cow's mobe. (Sigmund did all his Christmas shopping in one shop this year—he even got a mobile for Nan that has large numbers so she can see them and that plays "Amazing Grace.") I finally found it in her desk, looking pathetically untouched. She never uses it, so she'll also never know it's gone.

Read another page of *The Outsider* (to be honest, it's not exactly what I thought it would be from the title), **TWO** poems by this French guy Ms. Staples recommended, and the introduction to my yoga book tonight. The Dark Phase is going **REALLY** well. I almost can't remember what it's like to be a child anymore.

SUNDAY 21 JANUARY

Disha just rang. We had a v interesting conversation.
D wanted to know if I remembered her brother's friend
Elvin. (Disha's brother, Calum, is younger than Justin—
he's in the sixth form at our school—but he's about two
million years on in evolutionary terms. For one thing, he
can speak.) Disha says I've seen Elvin a couple of times.
He's the one Calum met on the special film course he's
taking. I said, "Blond?" Disha said no, he's the one with
the longish black hair who wears cowboy boots. I said,
"Oh, **HIM**!" Anyway, Disha was alone in the kitchen
with Elvin just now, and he'd been asking about **ME**!
Elvin's a naff name, but Disha and I agreed that he's pretty
good-looking. **ALSO** he wears black turtlenecks and his
hair is just long enough to make him look like a Beat poet.
(We discovered the Beat poets when one of them died and
Ms. Staples told us how they were an intellectual
movement and everything. Ms. Staples says they were
pissed off with the system and the middle-class lifestyle
long before the punks—True Artists always are.)

Disha says Elvin's at film school and he's already won a
prize for some film he made about cats (at least Disha thinks
it's about cats; she isn't **TOTALLY** certain). A filmmaker

is v cool—sort of a combination between an artist and a writer. I reckon I didn't really notice Elvin before because he's older. I know lots of girls like older men. (One of the maths teachers left over Christmas to fulfil her biological destiny and has been replaced by Mr. Plaget, who looks young enough to be a sixth-former except GORGEOUS, and you wouldn't believe how many girls who can't add up without a calculator are talking about doing A-level maths!!!) I, however, don't see the attraction. Older men make me sort of nervous. I think you have to suspect their motives. (I mean, why can't they get a woman their own age? Is there something wrong with them? Are they afraid of being with an equal? Do they think a younger girl would be easier to push around?) Elvin's different though (he's not that old—in fact he's probably the same age as Justin, but MUCH more mature). Disha and I agree that this is v exciting.

On a more mundane note, Sara Dancer's having second thoughts about DOING IT. She was talking to some girl who started having sex the day before she turned fifteen, and this girl reckons Sara should hold out for a bed as well as a real boyfriend. The first time this girl did it was in a garden shed (she had a rake handle in her back the whole time, but it was over pretty fast so it wasn't too bad). She says she's never done it without her clothes on or lying down—unless you count the back seat of her boyfriend's father's car, which none of us do. Sara says it doesn't sound much like in films. And I said it was just what I was always saying, wasn't it? Where's the *Romance*? Where's the *Passion*? Where's the overwhelming desire to merge your *Soul* (and a couple of body parts) with another?

MONDAY 22 JANUARY

Mentioned to David at lunch that I'm reading *The Outsider*. He was impressed. He said he admires Camus's clarity of intellect, philosophical optimism, and hopeful love of life. This doesn't sound much like the book I'm reading, but I said I did too. I reckon the optimism and hope must come after page three.

The yoga isn't as easy as it looks on the cover. I'm sure some of the positions are only possible if your bones are made of Plasticine or you're double-jointed or something. I was trying to do the Chakrasana (the Wheel, to the layperson) because it says in the book that it strengthens your thigh and stomach muscles (I reckon it beats going on another diet). I got into it OK, but then I got sort of stuck. It was either call for help or crash. I made the wrong choice. I screamed and Justin raced in, but of course he wasn't alone. He had his stupid camera with him. He snapped me just as I fell. He'd better hide that bloody thing, because if I get my hands on it I'm throwing it into the loo.

WEDNESDAY 24 JANUARY

IT HAS TO BE TOLD!
Five Reasons Why I Hate Catriona Hendley:
(1) She's **ALWAYS** had a big head because her mother writes for the *Guardian* and her father is some excruciatingly ginormous big deal at Channel Four.
(2) When we were in primary school, Catriona Hendley always made up dumb games for us to play, and I was always the dog.
(3) When we got to secondary school, Catriona Hendley asked me in front of everyone if I was a Taurus, but I didn't know anything about astrology then and I thought she said tourist and I said no, I was born in London. It took **EONS** to live it down.

(4) One day last summer we were all hanging out in the park and Catriona was telling some incredibly boring story. I was lying on the ground, watching the clouds, and I sat up to ask Disha something, and Catriona told me to lie back down and eat another **BAG OF CRISPS**! Like I'd already eaten one! In front of everybody! (Disha said that was not what Catriona said, but I think Disha was just trying to make me feel better. Disha's v loyal.)

(5) **CATRIONA HENDLEY'S AFTER ELVIN WHATEVER-HIS-NAME-IS!!!** I can hardly believe it myself. I mean, I know the world's a global village now, but it's still not **THAT** small. How does she even know him? He doesn't go to our school, she doesn't have an older brother, and *she's* not big mates with Disha. But the Eyes Don't Lie. There I was, minding my own business and waiting for Sara after school (Disha had to go to the dentist's), when who should come riding through the gates on his bicycle but Elvin! Now that I know he's interested in **ME**, his face has been burned into my brain and I recognized him immediately. He looked even cooler than I remembered. I reckoned he was meeting Calum, and I was just getting ready to go over and say hello in a hey-don't-I-know-you sort of way when Catriona Hendley came flying down the steps behind me like a bat out of hell (nearly knocking me over) and practically tackled him

as he got off his bike! If Catriona Hendley was built like a real woman (like some of us) and not a wood sprite, she would have floored him. Then she dropped her books. **ON PURPOSE!** (This is the twenty-first century. Can you believe it?) What could he do? He had to help her pick them up. And, anyway, she was practically standing on his feet so he didn't have much choice. This really isn't fair! He saw *me* first! If she'd batted her eyelashes any more, she'd've given him a **RASH**.

Rang Disha on the way home to tell her what happened. She's going to see what she can find out. I hope Nan's right and there is a hell, because it would really make my life to know that Catriona Hendley will be going there. Then we'd see how cool Ms. "So Trendy You Could Break Your Teeth on Her" really is.

THURSDAY 25 JANUARY

It took ages to get Mrs. Kennedy's twins to bed tonight. They must have visited their dad at the weekend, because they were all wound up about him. Dad this . . . Dad that . . . Dad . . . Dad . . . Dad . . . Boring or what? I think they're confusing him with someone who isn't doing time for armed robbery. Shane said their dad was coming home soon, and I reminded him that soon was nearly a year away. Children have no real sense of time. I had to keep interrupting my conversation with Disha to tell them to chill out, and it was a v important one. (Disha managed to get the information that Catriona Hendley used to live across the road from Elvin, so that's how they know each other—I'm not sure if I think this is good news or bad news.) I had to tell the twins to be quiet so many times that in the end Disha said she'd rather have a bath than listen to me screaming at Shane and Shaun, so we just hung up.

Rang Sara Dancer. Now she's having third thoughts. She says she's going to have to have sex sometime, so why not now? And also she says it's like putting off a haircut. I don't think so. There's nothing even remotely romantic about having your hair cut. Sara says maybe she'll meet somebody Saturday night. She's going to a party.

The MC was polishing off a bottle of wine when I got home. (On top of **EVERYTHING,** now she's started drinking as well! I don't know why, but it irritates me when she gets really inebriated.) First she told me what time it was and that these late nights had better not affect my schoolwork. Then she wanted to know where Mrs.

Kennedy went tonight. Doesn't she know they have pubs and cinemas in London and she doesn't have to go to Bristol for a drink after her computer class? I felt like telling her to get herself on Prozac **IMMEDIATELY**. It's bad enough she's always on at me, but extending her attacks to the neighbors can't be a good sign.

FRIDAY 26 JANUARY

I had a nightmare last night that Johnny Depp was my brother and Catriona Hendley was going out with him. Every time I turned a corner, there they were frantically exchanging saliva and flu germs. It was so scary, it woke me up. On the other side of love, the Mad Cow and Sigmund were shrieking at each other in the kitchen. You'd think they were trying to wake the dead the way they were carrying on. I wish they'd go back to just ignoring each other like they usually do. It was two in the morning, for God's sake! I mean, **REALLY**! One minute she's angry with poor Mrs. Kennedy for staying out after her class and ruining my sleep, and the next she's started World War III practically next door to my room! And also they're always telling me I never think about anyone else! I got my Discman and plugged myself in so I could get some sleep.

Tomorrow Disha's going with me to the yoga center to buy a mat so I don't slip over again. I have to pay for it myself, of course. Sigmund wouldn't give me the money because he says it'll just wind up with a bunch of plants on top of it like the piano. The Mad Cow can usually be worn down eventually, but she wouldn't cough up either this time. She says she paid for the leotard and the leggings, and that was enough. What did I think she was—MADE OF MONEY? I'm beginning to think she's made of toxic waste. I wonder if I should suggest hormone replacement therapy.

SATURDAY 27 JANUARY

OH MY GOD!!! YOU ARE NOT GOING TO BELIEVE THIS!!! Disha and I were coming out of the yoga center with my new mat (lilac because they didn't have black) and a Tibetan meditation CD (to help me get in the right mood, which is v important) when, as if drawn by the invisible forces of the universe, we happened to glance through the window of the veggie café next door. Sitting right in the middle of the room was Elvin. I was struck anew by how excruciatingly attractive he is. (I'm amazed it never really hit me before.) I swear, my heart **LITERALLY** skipped a beat (a sure sign of the first stirrings of *Passion*). And then my heart hit my kneecaps when I saw who was sitting with him. You could have knocked me over with a crisp wrapper. **OH YES!!!** None other than Catriona Hendley. She's like a germ the way she gets everywhere. Elvin and the Hendley were eating salads and having a v intense conversation. At least she was. She was leaning over so much she was practically in his lap! (It's just as well she doesn't have boobs or she would've suffocated him.) And then it hit me! Elvin and the Hendley have something in common besides being ex-neighbors! Everybody at school knows Catriona Hendley is the biggest vegetarian since the cow because she's always banging on about it (you'd think she'd invented it, the way she goes on). But I'd no idea about Elvin. I could see it all clearly. Catriona was trying to worm her way into Elvin's life through lettuce and herbal teas. I asked Disha why she hadn't told me about Elvin being a **VEGETARIAN** Serious Filmmaker, and she said that since she didn't hang around trying to see Elvin eat, she couldn't possibly know a thing like that, could she? She said she didn't think it was important anyway. (I'd like to know what she thinks *is* important!)

Nobody else at home tonight. Justin sloped off as soon as he'd stuffed his face, and then a while later Sigmund and

the Mad Cow rushed off shouting at each other. Isn't life
ironic? If I'd known I was going to have the flat to myself,
I'd've stayed home and enjoyed the luxury of all the peace
and quiet, but I'd already planned to go over to Disha's.
So, to take some advantage of this *Gift from the Gods*, I
helped myself to some of the politically correct bath oil
Sappho gave the Mad Cow for the winter solstice (which is
tested on nothing except chemists and is more expensive
than plastic surgery) and had a long soak before I went.
(Can you believe how childish my mother is? She hid the
bath oil behind the tinned vegetables because she thought
I'd never find it there!) The bath was bliss! Oh, how I long
to live on my own! When I can't sleep and I don't feel like
a *Romantic Fantasy*, I plan my entire flat. I choose the
furniture and the kitchen units, everything. I even plan
dinner parties.

SUNDAY 28 JANUARY

Desperate times call for desperate measures, and if starting
to *Fall in Love* with someone who is being stalked by
Catriona Hendley isn't desperate times I don't know what
is. So even though the book says that constructive spells (like
making someone have a hormone rush every time he sees

you) should be made during a full moon, I called an **Exploring Other Dimensions Night** last night. It was a new moon, so I decided to think laterally the way Sigmund is always telling me to. I reckoned we could trick the Other Dimensions into thinking there was moonlight. We rounded up every candle we could find (including a Frosty the Snowman one left from Christmas, a pack of birthday candles, and Calum's skull candle, which he wouldn't be needing since he wasn't home). Then we waited till Disha's parents went to bed so we didn't have to worry about being interrupted. That got us to one in the morning. Disha's mother is a phenomenal snorer (MUCH worse than Sigmund). Her snores are to ordinary snores what a nuclear bomb is to a slingshot. We left the transom over Disha's door open, and as soon as we could hear the earth-shaking snorts and wheezes that meant Mrs. Paski had passed out, Disha started lighting the candles while I started lighting the incense. The candles were going out as fast as she was lighting them, so we shut the window (Disha's father believes in AIR the way my father believes in Freud). Her room looked well wicked when we were done. Holding hands, we sat in the middle of the floor with our eyes closed. I started the incantation. "Pray to the moon when she is round—" But I didn't get any further, because Disha told me to be quiet and listen. I didn't hear anything. Disha said that was exactly what she meant. Her mother had stopped snoring! Disha has a more pessimistic nature than I do. She immediately decided that this meant her mother was getting out of bed to come and check on us. I said not necessarily (if I didn't have such an *Artistic Soul,* I might consider being a solicitor, since I also have a very logical mind). I said maybe Mr. Paski rolled her out of bed to shut her up. That's what the Mad Cow used to do to Sigmund (though lately she just makes him sleep on the couch, which is pretty bloody inconvenient if you want to sit up late watching a film).

Anyway, Disha started blowing out the candles in a frantic sort of way. We just got them all out when a sound even more horrific than Mrs. Paski's snoring shattered the peaceful silence of the night. Disha clutched my hand. Her palms were already sweating. "Oh my God!" she whispered. "We're being burgled." I told her that it definitely wasn't the house alarm. I'm an authority on house alarms. Ours was always going off till Sigmund ripped it out in a fit of temper, so I know what they sound like. This was more like an air raid siren. It wasn't easy getting to the light switch because of all the candles. Every time we took a step we knocked another one over. We were still groping around in the dark when Mr. Paski started running through the hallway shouting, "Fire! Fire! Everybody get out of the house!" We didn't need to be told twice. I once put the iron on my hand (I was thinking of something and wasn't looking), and Disha once set her shirt on fire with a candle, so we both knew the agony of burning flesh. We trampled over the candles and hurled ourselves through the door. Mrs. Paski had a blanket over her shoulders and a pair of high heels on her feet, but Mr. Paski was just wearing pajama bottoms, a ratty old Pink Floyd T-shirt, and one sock (God knows what he'd been up to!). We all ran into the road to wait for the fire engine. Every time we heard a siren, Mr. Paski shouted, "There they are!" But they weren't. Disha wanted to go back inside to save her new leather jacket, but her mother wouldn't let her. There was a bit of an argument about that, but then Mr. Paski started ranting and everyone finally shut up.

70

After a while Mrs. Paski said she didn't see any smoke. Mr. Paski told her that was the most dangerous kind of fire, the kind without smoke. Mrs. Paski pulled her blanket tighter and sniffed. She didn't smell smoke either. Mr. Paski said he smelled smoke. He asked me and Disha if we smelled smoke, and we said we guessed so since agreeing was a lot easier than disagreeing. Mr. Paski started standing on one foot. I wondered if he'd ever done yoga. After another while, one of the neighbors poked his head out of an upstairs window. Mr. Paski explained about the fire. The fire engine was there in minutes. Apparently, in all the confusion, neither of the parent Paskis thought of actually ringing the fire department!!! By then half the road was out on the street. Disha and I were just about to go next door for a cup of tea when a fireman came out of the Paskis' with Frosty in one hand and the skull in the other. Apparently the smoke from all the candles set off the alarm in the hall. Mrs. Paski mumbled something, and then she started laughing. Mr. Paski didn't laugh. (He didn't laugh later either, though Disha and I did.) Mrs. Paski told him to look on the bright side. If Calum had been home, he would have been filming the whole thing.

The MC and Sigmund weren't laughing either when I got home. Nobody told me, of course, but Nan broke her elbow falling off a bus yesterday. Apparently that's where they went rushing off to last night—the hospital. They had to put a pin in her elbow to hold it together. I didn't quite get the whole story. Sigmund and the Mad Cow were busy moving their stuff out of their bedroom so Nan could sleep in there, so all I got was a garbled account from Nan. She kept laughing and saying I should've seen the other guy (I presume she meant the pavement). They must've given her some heavy drugs for the operation. The major part of the story is that Nan has moved in with us until her elbow's healed enough for her to be on her own (which could take **MONTHS** considering how old she is). Her arm's all wrapped up in plastic like a hunk of meat. It looks really **GROSS**. Sigmund's wigged out completely. "Is this what Jesus would do if He broke His elbow?" he kept asking. "Move in with His son?" I hope he remembers this when he's old and feeble and wants to move in with me!

MONDAY 29 JANUARY

Sara Dancer's father twisted his ankle on Saturday night so Sara stayed home to look after him instead of going to the party. I think this may be an excuse. It's only an ankle, for God's sake.

Back in the land of the sexless, there was so much trauma at home last night because of Nan (Sigmund and the Mad Cow are both sleeping on the couch now, which is not exactly an optimum situation) that I forgot all about doing my spell again until I was getting ready for bed. It was raining, so I reckoned it didn't matter if the moon was full or not. I mean, who's going to see it anyway? I lit some candles and sat cross-legged on my bed in my underwear so I'd be more in touch with my primitive self. I closed my eyes and **REALLY** concentrated. At first I had to keep checking to make sure I was saying it right, but after a while I started to get into it. I swear I could feel the 𝔖𝔭𝔦𝔯𝔦𝔱 𝔬𝔣 𝔱𝔥𝔢 𝔉𝔢𝔪𝔞𝔩𝔢 𝔊𝔬𝔡𝔡𝔢𝔰𝔰 filling my room. I started rocking gently back and forth and chanting, "Queen of the Moon . . . Queen of the Sun . . . Queen of the Heavens . . . Queen of the Stars . . ." (I didn't plan to do this. It just happened! It was well wicked!!!) I forgot about who I was, and where I was. I was an Aztec maiden or an ancient druid. I was drifting in the cosmos like a particle of light, unfettered by the chains of the material world. At least I was until Nan screamed, "Praise be to Jesus! It's the devil's spawn!" I came back to Earth pretty sharply at that. My first real spell and I had a manifestation! The devil's spawn! How brilliant can you get? I opened my eyes, shouting, "Where? Where's the devil's spawn?" Turns out there wasn't any manifestation—Nan was actually talking about me! Can you believe it? Her own flesh and blood! I was well disappointed. It took **EONS** to calm her down (it's a good thing I wasn't naked). The Mad Cow put a sign on the bathroom door that says BATHROOM in case Nan gets confused again. I demanded that the lock on my door is fixed, but Sigmund isn't having it. He gave me twenty excruciatingly boring minutes on why he doesn't believe in locks (he doesn't know how to fix them himself and he's too cheap to pay someone else to do it is why).

TUESDAY 30 JANUARY

Late again for school. Mr. Wilkins gave me another detention. (According to the papers, teachers are leaving the profession **IN DROVES,** but not Mr. Wilkins, of course. Probably he knows he'd never get another job.)

Disha discreetly pumped Calum for more information on Elvin. (There's not a doubt in my mind that Disha is my cosmic sister. I know in my *Soul* it's no coincidence that we were born in the same year, in the same borough of the same city, and go to the same school.) Anyway, besides being a veggie, Elvin (according to Calum) is very concerned about the state of the planet. He feels filmmakers have a responsibility to show the world as it really is and to help protect it (so at least there's no danger that if I do *Fall Madly in Love* with him he'll go running off to Hollywood). Elvin's anti-hunt, anti-vivisection, and anti-international globalism (he's anti so much that even Sappho would approve). I asked Disha what international globalism was, since it's one of those terms that everybody uses but no one ever explains. I thought it might have something to do with the age of communication and being able to e-mail anywhere in the world in a second, but Disha said it had something to do with those riots they have every spring. So she isn't sure either. But whatever it is, Elvin was nearly arrested outside McDonald's at the riots last year. No wonder Catriona Hendley's after him. She's always protesting about something. She's practically London's answer to Joan of Arc. Besides all that, Elvin's taking some sort of Eastern martial arts course (for the philosophy, not the ability to break a brick wall with one hand, of course), but Disha couldn't remember which one. And also his star sign's Leo. I don't know anything about Leo. I'll have to ask Sappho.

The police were round at ours when I finally got home this afternoon! At first I thought they must be looking for Justin, but they were there to talk to Nan. Apparently she didn't fall off the bus; she jumped after some guy who'd grabbed her bag. She downed him, but he got away (*sans* said bag). The police were v impressed with her quickness of mind and body. Nan said it was the way she was trained in the war. She's obviously still suffering from the drugs.

GET THIS!!! Geek Boy overheard me telling Disha about the police and everything, and he said Nan **REALLY WAS** in the war. I said right, in an air raid shelter (which

D thought was v funny), but Justin said no, not in an air raid shelter, in France! He said she was some sort of spy. Disha and I nearly choked, we were laughing so much, but later I asked Sigmund and he backed Justin's story. He said not only did they give her a medal for bravery, but I'd seen it at least a million times because it's up on her mantelpiece, next to Grandad's ashes. So then I asked the MC, because although she has a lot of faults, winding me up isn't one of them. Plus she doesn't have a sense of humor. The MC said if I visited Earth more often, I might have some idea of what was going on around me. Which I took to be confirmation of Justin's story. My grandmother the spy. I **REALLY** can't believe it. The MC said that's because I think Nan was born **OLD,** which she wasn't. I said did she mean unlike *her,* and she said she took it back; I should stay on my own planet or she might have to kill me. Didn't I say she has no sense of humor?

WEDNESDAY 31 JANUARY

The Mad Cow was in a prize bitch mood this morning. If she got paid by the moan, she'd be a millionaire. All I did was ask where my black trouser-skirt was and she went mad. "I'm not your skivvy, young lady! If you want it washed, get off your bum and wash it yourself!" Justin shuffled in right then, asking about breakfast (one of the few verbal communications he can be relied on to make), and she rounded on him for a change. She told him he could do his own laundry from now on too. (How unfair is that? He only changes once every couple of weeks, whereas I change at least twice a day!) After that I didn't feel much like eating, so I made my escape. I was **HOURS** early, of course. It would've served the MC right if I'd been raped by some drug-crazed psychopath on his way home from a night of carnage. That's what I was thinking as I turned into the road the school's on. I was imagining my mother weeping on television, begging the nation to tell the police if they knew anything that could lead to the arrest of the heartless killer of her only daughter. I was practically crying myself. And what happened next? All of a sudden I heard a mobe go off behind me. It was playing the *Star Wars* theme song. The *Star Wars* theme song is definitely not something you'd expect a normal person to have on their mobe. It really took me by surprise, but I managed to calm myself down. (Psychopaths are like dogs —they can smell fear.) Besides, I was fairly certain a drug-crazed psychopath wouldn't remember to take his mobe with him. I mean, who would he call? Psychopaths don't have friends. And even if he did, what would he say? "Hi, I'm on the street and I'm just about to attack this attractive young woman with a bum like Jennifer Lopez's who's walking on her own." I looked round. It wasn't a mobe. It was a high-tech bicycle bell. And on the bicycle (which was also high-tech) was **ELVIN**!!! Electricity shot through me as if I were a metal pole (the metal pole of *Love*!). I couldn't believe it! What was he doing here? What if I hadn't left early? What if I'd been **LATE**? I half expected Catriona Hendley to drop out of a tree and ruin it all.

Elvin said, "Hi. It's Jan, isn't it?" I admitted to being Jan. He got off and walked the rest of the way with me. He was meeting Calum to give him something before school. I mentioned that Disha and I saw him in the café on Saturday, and he said we should have come in and said hello, so I explained that we were just going to our yoga class and didn't have time. He said he'd always been interested in yoga. I said it had changed my life. I told him we went into the café a lot (which is a slight exaggeration, but we do pass it quite often on our way to the video shop). I said we went there after our yoga class for herbal tea and stuff like that because there aren't that many places that cater for veggies. He said he didn't know I was a vegetarian too. I am now.

Bought a lock for my bedroom on the way home. If I'm going to really get into my yoga, I can't live in fear that

Justin's going to burst in to take more photos. It destroys my concentration.

Disha asked Calum if he met up with Elvin this morning, and Calum didn't know what she was on about. So Detectives Bandry and Paski now know that meeting Calum was just a feeble excuse. Elvin was there to see ME! I actually TINGLE when I think of it.

THURSDAY 1 FEBRUARY

I made my announcement about turning veggie at supper tonight (last night we had sausages, which is one of the few things the MC can actually cook properly, so I reckoned I might as well have one last meal as a meat eater). As per usual, I had to wait for Sigmund and his wife to finish their argument, but as soon as they took a break I pushed my plate away and went for it. "I can't eat this," I said. The Mad Cow turned her venomous gaze on me and wanted to know why not. Justin said he'd have it. Sigmund didn't say anything, because he'd already stormed off to go to one of his groups (Sigmund's got more groups than Columbia Records). I explained that I had become a vegetarian and would only be eating fish, chicken, and soya burgers from now on. "And you'll be cooking them yourself too," mooed the Mad Cow. "I'm not making special meals for *you*." I pointed out that her sister, Sappho, was a **VEGAN** and she didn't have to cook her own meals when she came round. The Mad Cow said I could go and live with her. And they talk about teenagers having attitude!

I was going to mention to Mrs. Kennedy that the twins have been a little overactive lately. But I never got the chance. As per usual, she was flapping all over the place getting ready and banging on about what a great person Sigmund is and how lucky I am to have him as my father. I always agree. I see no reason to burst her bubble.

FRIDAY 2 FEBRUARY

Cinderella Bandry (that's **ME**) was fixing herself a veggie burger for supper tonight when the oven mitt caught on fire. I reacted immediately. (I was v impressed!) Without a second's hesitation, I swung around and hurled the mitt into the sink. This was obviously the most intelligent thing to do, but of course the Mad Cow was in my way and the mitt hit her instead. You'd think I'd shot her (and except for a little singed hair she wasn't even hurt). Now she's changed her mind about me cooking my own food. Didn't I say she's menopausal? What more proof do you need, I ask you? She's up one minute and down the next like an oil pump.

I think I'm starving in the clinical sense. The incident with the MC and the oven mitt distracted me so much that the burger got burned and all I had for supper was vegetables. It's like living on water. But I'm not giving up. The Hendley has enough advantages with Elvin. I can't let her have that one too. And all I had last night was a cheese sandwich. I had to stop at McDonald's on the way to school this morning, I was feeling so faint. I ate two boxes of those chicken things (I couldn't eat duck—you know, because ducks are so cute—but chickens aren't very attractive so I reckon they're all right). But coming home on the bus tonight was this depressed-looking giant chicken (wearing Reeboks), and I wondered if it was some sort of sign and started feeling guilty.

Disha says she was once given a bag of baby carrots by a giant rabbit on Parkway. She says he was really grubby and there was even a stain on one of his ears. She threw the carrots away.

SATURDAY 3 FEBRUARY

Sigmund thinks my decision to show respect for other
animals and turn veggie is the sign he's been waiting for
that I'm not just getting older; I'm growing up as well.
He's delighted to see me thinking for myself and accepting
responsibility for my own life. (I don't understand why he
sounded so surprised.) Then he said that at least I was
doing better than the "bloody government." I bet the
bloody government isn't as hungry as I am though. I
finished off the shepherd's pie Mrs. Kennedy left for the
twins' supper on Thursday before I remembered about
being a vegetarian. I reckon it's all right though, because
she used mince and that doesn't really count as meat
either.

Disha said the giant chicken wasn't a cosmic sign. She said
he stands in front of that new chicken restaurant, handing
out flyers. I said I didn't think he really was a chicken (he
was wearing trainers!); I just thought maybe the universe
was trying to make me feel bad by putting him on my bus.
Disha said he was just going to work. Which is probably
why he looked depressed. I thought about that, and I can

definitely understand it. What must it be like, getting up every morning and putting on this bright yellow chicken suit, knowing tomorrow you're going to get up and do the same thing, and the next day, and the day after that . . . maybe for your whole life? (And I bet he's paid chicken feed!) I will never take a job as a giant chicken, no matter how desperate I am for cash.

Sappho came over this afternoon with her new girlfriend, Mags (she seems nice), and a Congratulations on Becoming a Vegetarian present for me. I was braced for some more feminist propaganda (never mind the winter solstice, for my birthday she gave me this huge book on the history of the suffragettes—she couldn't expect me to read it, so I reckoned I was meant to use it as a weapon), but what it was was this excruciatingly cool pair of purple combat trousers. Sappho said that every woman should own a pair, since they're in combat most of their lives. I would've liked them a teeny bit darker, but last time I commented on something Sappho gave me, she took it back, so I kept quiet. I think Mags must be a mellowing influence on Sappho.

Nan and Sappho are usually kept pretty much apart, because Nan thinks lesbians are really un-Christian, and she made sure Sappho knew how she felt right from the first time they met, which was at the parents' wedding. On that first, historic occasion, Sappho got melodramatic and stopped the band in midsong by loudly demanding to know why it was all right for Jesus to hang out with whores but not with gay people. On this occasion, however, Nan got a lot of sympathy from Mags for her broken arm, which kept her happy. And even Sappho was impressed with Nan's story (**HORRIBLY EXAGGERATED,** of course) of how she nearly caught the perpetrator because of her training in the war. Sappho said Nan was a closet feminist, and even Nan laughed.

So anyway, we got through giving me my present and showing Mags the flat without too much trauma. But as soon as we sat down for tea Sappho started banging on about female sexuality (not that anybody asked). It was so très boring. Especially if you've heard it all about six million times before. I was practically asleep when Nan suddenly shot to her feet, shouting, "I never had one of those things, and it didn't do me any harm!" It was pretty dramatic, with the sling and all. I had no idea what "things" she was talking about, but she definitely had my attention. Sappho put on her best professor of women's studies voice and said, "Mrs. Bandry, are you saying you've never had an orgasm?" This is not a word I've ever heard spoken aloud in our kitchen before. (In fact, I reckon it's not something that's happened very often in our house. If ever. The only sounds I've ever heard from the parents at night are either arguments or Sigmund's snores.) I wasn't alone. The Mad Cow spat the biscuit she was chewing right across the table. I thought she was going to choke to death. Mags asked if anybody wanted more tea.

SUNDAY 4 FEBRUARY

Disha and I went to Camden Market this afternoon. I got my nose pierced! I've been thinking about it for **EONS** and today I just went for it. Never mind the pain or possible disfigurement. (Even Catriona Hendley doesn't have her nose pierced!) Disha isn't sure how she feels about self-mutilation, so she just got two more holes put in each ear. We spent hours wandering around the market. It was well cool (aside from all the wicked clothes, we saw someone throwing up outside a pub, and someone else being dragged off by the police). I bought this Chinese skirt and these really cheap wind chimes (they're meant to be very calming, and with Nan in the flat I need all the calm I can get, so I bought three). Disha left me on my own while she went to get some fried noodles since I'm back on my diet today. Even though I don't eat

ANYTHING now that I'm a vegetarian I seem to have gained two pounds! (D says if crisps were made of pork I'd be all right.) Anyway, I was looking at the bowls on one of the stalls when the bloke said to me, "So what do you like?" I said I thought the blue fish bowl was nice, and he said that wasn't what he meant. I don't know why I always smile when someone says something I don't understand, but that's what I do. He smiled back. "Well?" he said. "Eees . . . weed. . . ? Maybe a hip girl like you wants something a little more exotic. . . ?" I couldn't believe it! It must be the nose ring. No adult has ever tried to sell me drugs before. Disha was furious that she missed it!

The only member of my family who noticed my nose ring was Nan. She thought I'd joined a pagan cult. She said she'd always known something like this would happen. Sigmund told her to put a sock in it; it was only a ring. And then all of a sudden Justin decided to join in. He wanted to know if I realized that the nose ring was a symbol of slavery and servitude. For cows and pigs, I said. Justin said for women too. Traditionally, if a woman wears a nose ring it means she's owned by a man. I said it was no such thing; it was a fashion statement. He said I'd be having myself circumcised next. (See what I mean by stupid? It's boys who get circumcised! Everybody knows that!) If you ask me, his parents should have thought about how their son would be affected by the ravings of a militant feminist during his formative years.

MONDAY 5 FEBRUARY

I couldn't believe it! I came out of art with Marcus and there was Elvin! As soon as I spotted him, I started laughing, even though Marcus wasn't saying anything funny. It was brilliant! Elvin looked well surprised. He'd come to see Mr. Belakis. (I can't believe Disha didn't find out that Elvin used to go to our school! She said I could have asked him that myself when I was talking to him the other day. Always an excuse!) Marcus wanted me to go to the high street with him, but I said I had things to do after school.

Later, I came out of the library just as Elvin walked past on his way out. I said I thought he'd be on his bike, and he said he wished that he was. He said it was the only way to travel in London, and I said too right. So when he asked me if I had a bike I automatically said yes (not a total lie— I used to have one; I just haven't had one for a while). And **GUESS WHAT**? He asked me if I wanted to go riding on the heath with him sometime! Do leaves grow on trees? I don't remember much after that, although I'm sure everything he said was v intelligent and witty. I know it sounds weird, but I almost wished he hadn't got on my bus. I really wanted to ring D and tell her all about it and everything he said, etc. But then he said he was dropping by Catriona's on his way home, and straightaway I wished he wouldn't get off.

You're not going to believe this, but Sappho says women *can* be circumcised! I said but we don't have a penis, and she said, "You really do live on your own planet, don't you?" (Ha-ha-ha, right? You can see why no one's ever accused feminists of having a great sense of humor.) I said well, we don't have penises, and she said maybe it would do me some good to pay some attention when people are talking to me now and then. Phoned Disha and she didn't know women could be circumcised either.

TUESDAY 6 FEBRUARY

Because I made One Little Comment about the nut cutlets she fed me last night (and they really did taste like cardboard), the Mad Cow went into one of her MEGA mood swings. After she calmed down she gave me thirty quid to buy myself some vegetarian food. I said I didn't know why she couldn't just pick up stuff for me when she's doing the carnivores' shopping and she said she has enough to do without trying to guess what I want to eat. Is that **LAZY** or what?

Disha went shopping with me after school. Neither of us has been in a supermarket for **EONS**. It was pretty horrifying. Not only is it as big as an airport terminal, but it was **ABSOLUTELY PACKED** with shoppers! Disha said you'd think they were giving the food away. We couldn't work out where all these people came from. Don't they have jobs? Don't they have lives? There's practically a whole aisle for crisps, a whole aisle for sweets, another aisle for biscuits, and yet another aisle for breakfast cereals. No wonder the Mad Cow spends hours getting the groceries. Disha said if she had to do the food shopping she'd probably spend the rest of her life trying to decide which packet of rice to buy. It took us an hour just to find where they hide the vegetarian stuff. After that it was easy since they hardly have anything. They've got more varieties of pizza than vegetarian meals. Then we had to queue for another eon. And what thanks do I get for wasting precious hours of my life doing the Mad Cow's job for her? **NONE!!!** She was all pissed off because I didn't bring back any change! I really should have a word with Sigmund about getting her on hormone replacement therapy. That or Prozac. I don't see how I can be expected to live with her lack of rational thought.

WEDNESDAY 7 FEBRUARY

I think Marcus thinks I like him (well, I do like him, but at the moment I'm not sure how much). Marcus, David, Sara, Lila, Nick, Disha, and me all went down to McDonald's after school (I had the fish thing, of course). We were sitting by the window when who did I see coming out of the video shop across the road? Calum and **ELVIN**! I wasn't sure what Elvin was doing outside McDonald's last spring that nearly got him busted, but I was pretty sure he wasn't queuing. And all of a sudden it hit me that I probably didn't want him to see *me* in McDonald's, even if I wasn't eating a hamburger. So I ducked under the table. Marcus (who was sitting next to me) looked down and asked me what I was doing. What I was doing at that very moment was kneeling in some ketchup trying to unhook my nose ring from his trousers without unhooking my nose as well. I didn't want to explain about Elvin, so I just said the first thing that came into my head. Which was that I wanted to give him a foot massage. And he said, "Why don't you come back to mine and give it to me there?" in a v suggestive way. I hope his mother can get the blood out of his khakis.

Revolting glop is oozing from the hole in my nose. I don't think this can be right. I just hope I don't have to be rushed to emergency in the middle of the night.

THURSDAY 8 FEBRUARY

TOTAL HUMILIATION! And it's all Mrs. Wist's fault. It was pissing down, so we got to stay in and play volleyball. What a treat! I told the old bag I was feeling crampy and wanted to go and get a pad, just in case, but she wouldn't let me leave the class. "I thought you had terminal cramps last week, Janet. How can you be getting your period *again*?" She was well sarky. Catriona Hendley laughed louder than anybody else. (Disha says I should've said that I was afraid of getting hit on the nose by the ball. Which would have been true. It already hurts like hell.) Anyway, I said that last week's cramps were a false alarm, but she wasn't having any of it. Mrs. Wist forced me to play, and of course I started bleeding like I'd been stabbed—right in the middle of the game. It was so gross! Blood was dripping down my leg. Everybody started shrieking. You'd think that with PE being the last class of the day, Mrs. Wist would have let me go home after that, to avoid the rush, but **OH NO**, she let me go and get a pad and clean up and all, but then she made me stay right to the gruesome end. I didn't want to go on the bus because I was feeling really stressed by then, so I went to Disha's to call the Mad Cow to come and get me. And who do you think was sitting in the kitchen, eating a cheese sandwich? Elvin! Who else? Of all the billions and billions of people in the world—many of whom I wouldn't mind seeing me traumatized and smelling like something slaughtered—it had to be him. I would've swooned, but I was on automatic panic. This was my big chance! My chance to sit down and have a cheese sandwich with one of the most desirable men in London while we discussed the merits of being vegetarian. Only I Couldn't Take It because I felt so gross. I didn't even say hello. I just turned straight round and collided with Disha. I nearly trampled her getting out of the room. What a day!!!

Three Reasons Why Disha Paski's *My Best Friend:*
(1) She's intelligent and loyal.
(2) We're into all the same things.

(3) Disha told Elvin that the reason I ran off like that yesterday was because I suddenly remembered it was the afternoon I worked in the local Oxfam shop. It was a pretty brilliant lie. She said he was suitably impressed, being the serious sort. I just hope he never asks me where the shop I work in is, since I haven't a clue. Except for when the MC used to take me to charity shops when I was little and didn't know any better, I've never been to one in my life. They smell. And also Siranee's sister's friend got bugs from a secondhand jumper once.

FRIDAY 9 FEBRUARY

I think I may start keeping a list of Most Unromantic Sexual Encounters. Forget the garden shed and the back of a car. Boris Becker knocked up some model in a broom cupboard. I couldn't believe it either, but it was on the radio so it must be true. He was in some well posh Japanese restaurant, and between courses or something he followed this model into the cupboard, and nine months later he's a dad. Boris Becker! He's always dressed in white, so you sort of think of him as a good guy. I'm beginning to think that if you're going to have a role model you should probably pick someone who's already dead so they can't disappoint you. Disha says not to forget President Clinton when I start my list. She says she knows power's meant to be a turn-on, but she doesn't think the Oval Office with armed guards outside and all those phones would put her in the mood.

Lila's parents are going away for a romantic weekend so Lila's decided to have a valentine party tomorrow night, despite what happened last time. I wish Sigmund and the Mad Cow would go away for a **LONG** romantic weekend, but even if they weren't **AT WAR** and might possibly do such a thing, they'd have to take Nan with them, so there's no use hoping. Marcus asked me if I was going to Lila's and I said yes, of course—even though I have **NOTHING** to wear. He's going to pick me up so we can walk over together. I said that was great. I told Disha to meet us at mine.

Disha's had a **BRILLIANT** idea! She thinks I should send Catriona Hendley a valentine and make her think it's from David. Lila, who's a v good friend of Catriona's, told Disha that Catriona used to have the hots for David, but even though he hangs out with her a lot (because her parents own a heated pool and a snooker table!), he's never asked her out. That should take Catriona's mind off Elvin for a bit. Disha said what we should do is write a D on the card, and then partly cover it over with a sticker so it looks like he started to sign it and then tried to hide it. Then she said we should send David one from Catriona too. Disha shows a remarkable talent for subterfuge.

Even though my nose still looks a bit red and has a tendency to leak, I went over to Disha's this afternoon because Elvin was going to be there. I was very cool. This time I didn't run out of the kitchen; this time I sat down. Elvin and Calum are going to make a film together, probably in the summer if everything works out right. (Apparently there's much more to making a movie than putting film in the camera.) They talked a lot about it. I think it's sort of a documentary about people. We fixed toasted cheese sandwiches. Elvin and I made a great deal of eye contact. He even asked me a couple of questions: why I became a vegetarian, what my favorite subject is, and if I have a brother (because the meat industry is irresponsible and motivated only by profit, which is what Sappho always says; art and English, but I wish we had a film course; and, yes). He said he thought he'd heard of my brother. I told him that was virtually impossible. I'm well chuffed that I had the sense to hide in McDonald's, even though I have no idea how to get ketchup out of my combat trousers.

David rang for a chat. As you know, I usually flirt with David, but I was still thinking about Elvin and didn't have the energy. It's funny, isn't it? When you have no single object of your desire, you can flirt with anyone, but as soon as your heart begins to yearn to see that one face, you lose interest in the others. At least that's the way it is for me. And also my nose really hurts. You don't feel like flirting when your nose really hurts.

96   SATURDAY 10 FEBRUARY

Went shopping with Disha this afternoon. She wanted to get something to go with her red skirt for the party tonight (we reckon we can be exempt from the DP just this once—after all, even Great Artists and Writers do *Fall in Love*, even if it's only **TRAGICALLY**). I, of course, could buy **NOTHING**. I have to save all my money for a bike, and no one else would give me any. (Not even Justin. He's left the photos of Jocelyn and Robert Bandry sleeping at Andrew's, so it's my word against his.) I offered to do errands for Nan for a nominal charge, and she accused me of being worse than a moneychanger in a temple. I even tried to borrow a tenner from Justin, but he wasn't having it either. He said that I still owed him fifty quid from the summer. I pointed out that I'd only borrowed a fiver that time. He said it was fifty quid with interest. (Rest assured, the skies over London will be choked with pigs before he sees any of that!!!) Anyway, Disha and I went to the West End. I was so distraught over my poverty that I forgot to bring my mobe and Disha's was at home charging, so she had to use a phone box to ring her mother and find out what it was she was meant to pick up for her. You couldn't even see out of the box, there were so many cards plastered all over the glass. And they're not like minicab cards (you know, name, phone number, and maybe a drawing of a car). They're full-color photographs with whips and stuff like that. Disha said she doesn't know why they bother putting porn magazines on the top shelf of the news agent's when the phone boxes are wallpapered with the same sorts of pictures. She said Sappho must never come to the West End, because if she did there wouldn't be a box left standing. I asked Disha if she thought they were **ALL** prostitutes, or if some of them really were masseuses and personal trainers. Disha said she hoped I was joking. It was just that there seemed to be **SO MANY**. Disha said well, there would be, wouldn't there? You don't need any qualifications, you make more than you would working in Woolworth's, and you don't have to pay tax. All you have to worry about is not catching some fatal disease or being beaten up or murdered. I think prostitution in general has to go on my Most Unromantic Sexual Encounters list. It makes the giant chicken job look good if you ask me. There's obviously a lot more to sex than you'd think. Or a lot less.

Walked past a bike shop on the way home. I couldn't believe the prices! I could buy a motorized scooter for that! Disha said I should look for a secondhand one in Loot.

When Sigmund saw the hole in my door where I tried to put on the lock, he lost it completely, as per usual. Yadda yadda yadda. It's hard to believe he gets paid to **LISTEN** to people. I've never heard him keep his mouth shut for more than two seconds. He says I've **TOTALLY** ruined the door and that now he'll have to get a new one—and God Knows How Much That's Going to Cost. I said to make sure he got one with a lock.

I practically rubbed my fingers to the bone trying to get the ketchup out of my new trousers, but you can still see it, so I bought a bottle of black dye to hide the stain. It looks pretty easy. You just dump it all in the washing machine.

SUNDAY 11 FEBRUARY

Marcus was late picking us up last night, which was just as well since I had to change **FIVE** times before I found something presentable to wear. I tried on the Chinese skirt I got in the market, but it must've shrunk or something because it was too tight. Ditto my pink Lycra. Even Disha said I looked like an overstuffed sausage. I can't possibly be gaining weight, even though I'm not **STRICTLY** on my diet anymore because I don't really eat anything but vegetables. Finally remembered the MC's black silk skirt (mercifully she was out), which is both casual and sophisticated and went **PERFECTLY** with the bat top.

When Marcus arrived he was wearing a pink bow tie and carrying a single red rose. (Even Disha said he looked pretty good.) I acted overwhelmed. "For **ME**?!! Oh, you shouldn't have!" He said, "Sweets for the sweet; roses for the thorny." (He can be pretty funny.) Marcus said that if he'd known he was escorting two devastatingly beautiful women to Lila's and not just one he would've bought another rose. He reckoned he could've got a deal on two. We were just about to leave, when David turned up.

(I forgot he also said he wanted to walk over with me.) David was wearing a red shirt (no tie), but he had a rose too (they must've been giving them away at the end of the road). I think he thought Marcus's rose was for Disha, because he whipped it out of my hand and thrust it at her. And then he gave me the one he'd brought.

It wasn't until we got to Lila's that I understood why I'd been **SO PARTICULAR** about what I was wearing. My psychic self must've been picking up messages from the Earth Goddess because guess who was already there when we arrived! Yes! Oh **YES YES YES**!!! Fate is with me! It was none other than Elvin Whatever-His-Name-Is. My heart did a double flip and the rest of the room faded around him. I was glad the lighting was low, because I could feel myself blushing (which is something I usually only do when I'm out in public with members of my family). Elvin was talking to Catriona. (Of course! She would've known he was going to be there, wouldn't she? She's not one to miss an opportunity! It doesn't even have to knock. She sees it coming, opens the door, and hauls it in.) There were a bunch of other people with them at the back of the room. I pretended not to see them and gave Marcus my jacket to stick in the bedroom. David said he'd do it, and whipped it out of Marcus's hands. Marcus snatched it back and marched off. Within seconds, Elvin was coming towards us (towards me!). I was practically *Swooning with Happiness,* but I didn't let it show. Still acting like I hadn't seen Elvin, I stood as close to David as I could without actually hugging him. (If a bloke's interested, he'll be even more interested if he thinks he's not the only one. I'm not sure where I read that, but Sara Dancer says it's true.) It sort of worked. It was definitely a V AWKWARD moment. Only it wasn't Elvin who started to bristle like a dog that's just seen another dog — it was David. I could feel him get taller. And then Marcus came back and latched himself on to my other side. I felt like I was wedged between two Roman columns or something. Elvin (being a sensitive Leo) must've realized that D and M were being all male territorial because I've been friends with them for so long, because after the usual friendly greetings, instead of bringing up the bike ride or anything like that, he asked me if Marcus was my brother! Marcus wanted to know if he *looked* like my brother, and Elvin said he wouldn't know since he's never met my brother. Elvin and I thought that was v funny. As soon as Elvin went back to Catriona and her motley crew, Marcus asked who he was. Then he mumbled something about Elvin always hanging around. Disha and I watched Catriona and David (subtly, of course) to see if they made eye contact or anything. **AND GUESS WHAT?** It was all we could do not to laugh out loud! David kept looking over at her so much that he barely kept up with the conversation, and she cast more than one thoughtful look his way too. I suppose it was just as well for everybody's concentration that Elvin left early and Catriona left the room (though not the building, sadly). But despite the fact that Elvin left really early and I didn't get a chance to talk to him again, I had a pretty good time. At Lila's Halloween party the only person who danced with me was her cousin from Glasgow, whose concept of dancing was to jump straight up and down in the air like a Jack Russell. This time, however, I had two boys to dance with—usually, as it turned out, together. They're both **REALLY** good dancers. I found it very exhausting, though, so when Marcus went into his John Travolta routine, and then David went into his, I slipped away and sat down. It took them **EONS** to notice.

Mr. Burl next door was backing his scooter out of his front garden as we got to my house. I closed the gate for him. Then Marcus and David came in for a cup of tea. After they left I told Disha how hostile Marcus and David were to Elvin. Disha thinks they both thought they were going to the party with me. I said she was mad. I'd remember if one of them asked me out. Anyway, what about David and Catriona? Their eyes were drawn to each other like magnets. Disha said she'd forgotten about David and

Catriona. So maybe it was just Marcus after all. D said it would serve me right for practically licking his boots in McDonald's the other day.

The Mad Cow's having dinner with Sappho and Mags, Sigmund's grouping (left-handed redheaded dyslexic unwed fathers with one blue eye probably), and Justin's gone out, leaving me grandmother-sitting, **AS PER USUAL**. Fortunately Nan's nodded off in front of the telly, so now's my chance to dye my combats without her telling me how Jesus would do it.

MONDAY 12 FEBRUARY

Found the roses Marcus and David brought under the table in the hall, still in their wrappers but already withered and dead. *Love* and 𝔇𝔢𝔞𝔱𝔥. I reckon they're the two greatest themes in art and literature—as well as in life. And it made me realize how short life really is. We are all born to die (I don't know if some poet wrote that line before I did, but I think it's pretty good). At least the roses had their moments of beauty. (That's more than my mother ever had!) I took a couple of petals to press in my diary, and then I chucked them in the bin.

Last night I dreamed that I was at this barbecue (like in Texas or somewhere like that). There were whole cows turning over the coals. And you should've seen the burgers! They looked like meteors! I was sweating when I woke up. It's weeks since I became a vegetarian, and all I've had besides vegetables is fish and chicken (and that little bit of mince). And my parents think I don't stick to anything!

There must be something wrong with the washing machine. The combats didn't exactly come out the way I thought. The trousers are brilliant, but the stitching didn't take the dye, so I've got these really cool **BLACK** trousers with almost **WHITE** stitching. It is v passé. And not exactly my image.

TUESDAY 13 FEBRUARY

The Mad Cow nearly got arrested in the supermarket for nicking a birthday card that somebody left in her trolley (at least that's her story!!!). Apparently there was a **MEGA** scene with the manager, and **HUNDREDS** of shoppers were standing around watching. Sigmund said considering how much money she spends there each week they should be giving her **BOXES** of free cards, not persecuting her. The MC said it was nice of him to take her side for a change, and they nearly got into another row. (I'm beginning to think that rowing's what they do instead of having sex.) Justin said the MC was really unlucky to get the only conscious security guard in London. Nan said she should sue for defamation of character (which, let's face it, would be **REALLY** hard to prove). The MC says she can never go back there again, in case somebody recognizes her. I told her not to worry about that since nobody remembers what women her age look like. And then she got angry with **ME**!!! She says she hopes she's still alive when I'm her age so at least she can die laughing.

D reckons I can cover up the white stitching on the combats with a laundry marker. If you ask me, she should consider a career in fashion. She has a real talent.

VALENTINE'S DAY

To celebrate this day of *Love,* the boys who sit at the back in Mrs. Gumpta's maths class let loose a bunch of inflated rainbow-colored condoms while Mrs. G was writing on the board. She thought they were balloons. It was excruciatingly hilarious. Disha said you could bet that if we'd had Mr. Plaget, he would've known what they were!

I GOT MY FIRST VALENTINE! It was waiting for me when I got home this afternoon. It's one of those really naff ones with a red satin heart trimmed with lace. I love it! I put it on my bureau so the Mad Cow will see it when she patrols my room and know that someone loves me. That should wind her up. Here she is, finishing her life as a woman, and I'm just about to begin mine. Dare I hope that my secret valentine is Elvin? Was that moment when he smiled at me in Disha's kitchen the moment when he thought, I think I'm *Falling in Love* with Jan?

THURSDAY 15 FEBRUARY

So what's the **FIRST** thing I see when I get to school this morning? Nothing less than Catriona and David chatting nonchalantly just inside the gate!!! Were they discussing their valentine cards, one wonders? I gave them both a **BIG** greeting, and David got a distinctly pink tinge to his complexion, as though I'd come across them snogging or something. Naturally I acted like I didn't notice. David did eat lunch with us, but I'm sure it was just to divert suspicion. He was definitely preoccupied, and even though Marcus had the rest of us in stitches, David hardly cracked a smile.

Since no one sent her a valentine, the MC bought herself a bottle of sparkling chardonnay. It didn't help her mood any, though. She was all sarky because I was going to Mrs. Kennedy's (as per usual!) and wanted to know if The Woman ever stayed home. I said what happened to Female Solidarity and being supportive of single mothers? The MC said maybe I should ask Mrs. Kennedy about Female Solidarity. God knows what she was on about. She really is gong through the CHANGE—from human to witch.

The MC must've gone round to Sappho's for more wine, because she wasn't in the flat when I got home from Mrs. Kennedy's. Nan was asleep at the kitchen table. She's not getting older; she's turning into a cat. No matter where you put her, she nods off. Even in the middle of supper (though not before she's said grace)! Disha says it's better than her grandmother. Her grandmother doesn't remember anything unless it happened seventy years ago. She calls Disha Paula and is always asking her if she liked the chocolates.

FRIDAY 16 FEBRUARY

Caught David and the Hendley with their heads together in the library today!!! Made a point of going over to say hello. Did David look **EMBARRASSED** or what? He gave me some crap about history homework. Yeah, right. Like I was born yesterday.

The Mad Cow had another **major trauma attack** tonight because her whites came out gray. Sigmund and Justin had vanished, as per usual, and Nan was passed out in front of the telly (also as per usual), so she came straight for me. She wanted to know what I'd been doing in the washing machine. "Nothing," I said. "Washing clothes." She started waving a finger in front of my face. Hysterically. "Then what's this, Janet? What's this?" she kept shrieking. It was black dye. She said if this was my clever way of getting out of doing my own laundry, I could forget it. She suggested I read **ALL** instructions before I did anything. She said if it **EVER** happened again, she was going to send me to Indonesia to work in a factory until I'd earned enough to buy a new machine. She reckons it would take till I'm thirty.

Everybody else had spaghetti Bolognese for supper tonight, but all I had was a cheese sandwich because Nan threw out the soya mince. She thought it was dog food and we don't have a dog. How is it possible that I'm related to these people? I hope I'm not getting anemic.

Found myself in the kitchen with my parents' other child tonight. I was ignoring him as usual when he suddenly told me I should give the MC a break. I said what? Her leg? Her arm? Her neck? He said it's not a joke. Can't I see the state she's in? I said it would be pretty hard for me to miss it, since I'm the one who gets most of her shit. Thank God, our conversation got cut short by Sigmund barging in, looking for the corkscrew (the MC was over at Sappho's again so he couldn't ask *her*). Justin didn't even look at him; he just mumbled something about it being about time that I joined the human race, and left the room.

SATURDAY 17 FEBRUARY

I woke up this morning looking like I'd been bitten by the King Kong of mosquitoes. My whole nose is red now. And swollen! The Mad Cow says it's infected and made me take the ring out. Thank God it's half-term or I might end up going to school with a bag over my head like Katie Jamers did that time she dyed her hair pink and her father went **INSANE** and **SHAVED IT ALL OFF**! Sappho gave me one of her herbal remedies for my nose. At least it smells OK.

Since looking like something deformed has made it impossible for me to go out in daylight, I read another couple of pages of *The Outsider* and did some yoga. I was feeling in a pretty reflective mood after that, so I wrote a poem about being Here while everyone else is There. Disha said it was v deep, which is what I thought. So maybe it was important for my nose to go septic for me to assimilate what the DP has taught me so far.

SUNDAY 18 FEBRUARY (Sara Dancer's advice about locked doors proves prophetic!!!)

Three Reasons Why I Hate My Brother:
(1) He's ugly and stupid.
(2) He tore up my best coloring book when I was four.
(3) This afternoon I was practicing yoga to my new CD (the chanting does help, though there's a bit when they suddenly start blowing trumpets and banging cymbals that

comes as a surprise the first time you hear it) when the stereo just stopped playing. I wasn't going to go through all the bother of finding a new fuse and putting it in and all that, so, since Justin wasn't home, I went to his room (otherwise known as the Black Hole) to borrow his stereo, which is like going into a house where someone's just died of bubonic plague. His room isn't just untidy— it **SMELLS**. I couldn't see his stereo, so, holding my nose and trying not to gag or touch anything with my skin, I started kicking piles of clothes aside. And what do you think I found? **MY LEOPARD-PRINT BRA!!!** That's what I found!!! Are you revolted? Multiply that by about a trillion and you'll know how I felt! I picked it up with my sleeve and brought it downstairs to show the Mad Cow. (I don't want to think about what he was doing with it!) The MC was less than horrified. She said there's probably nothing unhealthy about it (there is for **ME!**), and that Sigmund will "have a word with Justin." Well, that should help. (Sigmund never has less than a thousand words with anyone, and Justin will stop listening completely after "talk to you.") And also she refuses to buy me a new bra. She says I'm being melodramatic and I should just wash it. She says it probably just got mixed up in the laundry, which is another good reason we should each do our own. I may have to burn it.

There must be more to Sappho's picking-wild-sage-when-the-moon-is-full routine than I thought. The swelling's gone down and my nose has stopped aching.

Disha was suitably **AGHAST** when I told her what Geek Boy did. She says it just proves that you never really know anyone, not even the people who are closest to you. There are always depths. D says it's sort of scary when you realize that **EVERYBODY** has a secret, inner life. I said not everybody. As the child of Robert and Jocelyn Bandry I can say that with **CERTAINTY**. And as far as Justin goes, I don't know if I consider nicking my bra a **DEPTH** exactly, even if it is true that I wasn't expecting it. It's more like a **Cesspool of Shallowness**.

MONDAY 19 FEBRUARY (Half-term. Can I use the break? Do I need to breathe?)

Sigmund made Justin apologize for nicking my bra. If you count uttering one word ("Sorry") from behind a camera an apology. Justin said it was Andrew's idea. (Andrew is the fourth reason I hate my brother.) According to Justin, they just wanted to see how it worked. What for? Are they planning to wear one? I'm going to make a list of every bra I own so I can check whether any go missing in the future.

The Mad Cow and Nan were all atwitter when I got home from Disha's this afternoon. I reckoned there must've been another excruciatingly exciting incident in the supermarket, so I wasn't really paying attention till I heard Nan say that she thought it might be a good idea if we set up a neighborhood watch. Nan said she doesn't know what the world's coming to. In her day (like she can remember that far back!) people looked out for each other and knew how to take care of themselves. I thought Sigmund must've had another car stereo nicked (number five!), but it turned out that Mr. Burl next door was robbed. Somebody took his scooter last Saturday night! My mobe was charging, so I raced to the kitchen phone to tell Disha that we'd actually witnessed a robbery in progress. Disha said hadn't she said Mr. Burl looked like he'd lost some weight? I said no. (I certainly don't remember that.) She thought maybe the police would want to question us. The only person who wanted to question me was the Mad Cow. She'd been listening to my whole conversation, of course (I couldn't have less privacy if I lived in a doorway). The MC was **HORRIFIED** that I actually *saw* someone going off with Mr. Burl's bike and didn't say anything. I asked her what she wanted me to say. Anyway, how was I meant to know it wasn't Mr. Burl going for a moonlit ride? It was dark. She said she hoped I realized that at some point in time I was going to have to take up residence on Earth, and advised me against going into any career that required even an insignificant amount of thought.

TUESDAY 20 FEBRUARY

Another v interesting day!!! Went shopping for general maintenance supplies (shampoo, conditioner, etc.), and who should I spy with my little eye but Catriona and David! They were coming out of the record shop near the tube. They weren't holding hands, but they were walking V CLOSE!!! I really am a creature of impulse, because I suddenly decided to follow them. They strolled along just looking in windows for a bit, and then they went into Woolie's, Agent Bandry right behind them. Woolie's was crowded and it wasn't easy to keep them in sight and stay out of sight at the same time. I was sidling past the kitchen stuff when I realized David and Catriona weren't the only ones being followed!!! I was being closely observed by a youngish man in a Nike sweatshirt. I dived down the sweets aisle, and he popped up at the other end. I knew instantly that it wasn't lust or anything like that, though.

He had undercover security guard written all over him. The last thing I wanted was to follow in the footsteps of Jocelyn Bandry and get accused of shoplifting. Especially with the Hendley about (spreading sensational news stories is in her blood after all). I suppose I could simply have left, but I didn't think of that until later. Instead I was attacked by genius once again! I went straight to the manager and told him a pervert was following me around the store. Naturally, the manager didn't want to admit that it was the store detective, so we got into a v intense discussion. Perhaps acting is my real calling, because I definitely got into my role of Victimized and Innocent Young Woman Alone. The manager finally offered me a five-pound gift voucher to appease me, which I generously accepted. The downside was that by the time I returned to my quarry they were gone. Decided to save the voucher for Nan's birthday.

Came home to find the female parent **IN MY ROOM**! She was lying on my bed! I was highly indignant, I can tell you. Not only was this a **MAJOR** breach of my privacy, but her eyes were all red and she was sniffling like she was coming down with something. She'd better not be infecting me with her germs. She said she was taking a break from Nan, but I know her better than that. She knows I got a diary for the winter solstice, and she probably wants to read what I say about her (though I can't imagine why, since even **SHE** must realize it isn't going to be good!). Time for a move!

Sigmund and Nan had an argument tonight. For a change! This one was about war as a method of settling differences. Sigmund doesn't think it's what Jesus would do. Nan said the Bible said an eye for an eye and a tooth for a tooth. Sigmund said it also said turn the other cheek. Nan stomped off muttering that the Word of God is the Word of God, and Sigmund shouted after her, "Even when It contradicts Itself?" The Mad Cow told him if he didn't stop winding Nan up she was going to kill the two of them. I know she was only kidding, but Disha's words from the other day came back to haunt me, and I stared at her for a few seconds like I'd never seen her before. Maybe D's right and **EVERYBODY**—even my mother—has an inner, secret self. Maybe, deep down in her inner, secret self, Jocelyn Bandry (primary school teacher and graduate of the St. John Ambulance first aid course) really would kill someone. People do, don't they? You see it on the news all the time. The neighbors are always well shocked. Usually it's a man slaughtering his wife and children, but it could go the other way, couldn't it? And even if the MC's not a serial killer waiting to happen, lots of housewives go into prostitution for extra money (this is well documented in films and TV programs). And there was this suburban wife and mother in America who it turned out was wanted by the FBI for being a terrorist in her youth. I know none of these seem likely for my mother, but it did make me think. I must've got lost in my thoughts because she suddenly started shrieking, "And what are *you* looking at?" So I said I was just wondering if she *really* had the potential to murder someone, and she said not to provoke her. I beat a hasty retreat, but I couldn't stop thinking about how you never **REALLY** know **ANYONE**. It's all through literature and history. Betrayal. Treachery. Deception. It's even in comic books and films, for God's sake! After a while, though, I got really **tired and depressed** thinking about all this so I went and watched telly with Nan for a while, but her soap was pretty **RIFE** with betrayal and deception too (who knew the Dark Phase was going to be **THIS** dark?!!), so I rang Disha. D says Shakespeare was totally obsessed with treachery, betrayal, and deception. She says it just proves we really are probing the **DEPTHS** of human experience. She says now she **TOTALLY** understands that poem about ignorance being bliss. And I said our *Souls* must be even *Deeper and More Creative* than we thought. D agreed. Now I feel oddly at *Peace*. I reckon we've reached another spiritual plateau!!!

WEDNESDAY 21 FEBRUARY

Justin has a black eye. He won't say how he got it. Probably walking into a lamppost or something. He's always hurting himself (last time it was a broken ankle). Not only is he the clumsiest thing on two feet, but he's practically comatose most of the time. Sigmund said he hoped Justin wasn't doing anything dangerous. Like what? Eating hamburgers? Crossing against the light? (This isn't exactly the young Indiana Jones we're talking about here. Justin hasn't even ridden a bike since he was hit by a police car.) Nan said thank God he wasn't hurt worse, and the Mad Cow muttered something about nothing being more important than human life (although I can think of several things that are more important than Justin's life).

THURSDAY 22 FEBRUARY

Made another attempt at my story for the school mag this morning, but writing is **A LOT** harder than it looks. I was pretty relieved when David rang up. He was bored too. So in the end I hung out with Marcus, David, Siranee, Disha, etc. at David's. I took the opportunity to try and get some information out of him about what's happening with

Catriona when we had a few minutes alone. I started out by asking him if he got any valentines and he actually blushed! Busted!!! (It was really *v Sweet and Endearing*. Like when you see some guy built like an American football player with a baby. I don't know why that should seem so sweet—I see dozens of women with babies every day and all I think is that's their youth and figure gone.) I said I got one too, to encourage him, and he didn't say anything. Then I asked him who he thought his was from, and he smiled (he has one of those v attractive lopsided smiles) and said he had an idea but he wasn't going to say. I was about to start wheedling when the others came back. Better luck next time.

Disha said did I notice that Marcus and David seemed a bit cool to each other, and I said no. D said **REALLY?** I asked her if she was trying to make some point, and she said no, she was just saying because the DP has got her into the habit of thinking and noticing things. I reminded her that we're meant to be noticing things with profound significance, not mundane details.

I've spent a lot of the half-term going through all the possibilities, and I really think my valentine must have been from Elvin. It was too soppy for Marcus. And I **KNOW** I'm right about David being interested in the

Hendley. Who else is there? This is the first time anyone's sent me one, and it's the first time I've known Elvin. The logic seems pretty irrefutable to me. So, since he obviously is interested in me (having more or less said so), I've decided to be one of those new women you're always reading about in the color supplements and not wait for him to ring me about the bike ride. After all, maybe he forgot. He is a filmmaker. You wouldn't expect Spielberg to remember he once asked you to go on a bike ride, would you?

I don't think being twins can be healthy. Either S&S don't speak to me at all because they live in their own little Twin World, or they won't shut up and talk in stereo. Tonight they were banging on about their father again. Apparently he's bigger than my father, stronger than my father, cleverer than my father, and even better looking than my father. God they're exhausting! I ask you, who would be young? How tedious and infantile their minds are. I tried to ignore them. After all, I couldn't really argue with them—they are mere children—and, anyway, since I've never met their dad (because he's been inside all the time I've known Mrs. Kennedy) they may be right as far as I know. (The DP is also helping me develop an open mind.) Then Shane said their dad could beat my dad up, and Shaun said too right. I asked them why he would want to do that, and they said **BECAUSE**. Could I ever have been like that? It really doesn't seem possible. Sigmund was still up when I got back, so I told him how weird they've been lately. I reckoned, since he's Mrs. Kennedy's therapist and all, he'd be interested, and he was. He went into this long yadda yadda yadda about the way twins relate, and their imaginations, and how you can't really believe much they say, especially twins who have been through as much as Shane and Shaun and have to pretty much make up a father. And he thinks I talk a lot!!! As per usual, I was v sorry I'd brought it up. I said all I really wanted to know was if he thought they could be on medication. Sigmund said the only person he suspects of being on medication is me. You can see what I'm up against. And he expects me to have serious conversations with him!

FRIDAY 23 FEBRUARY

Since the McDonald's incident, I've been reluctant to hang out with the boys anywhere too public, just in case we run into Elvin (which, with my **LUCK**, would be bound to happen), because even though it does men good to think that other men are interested in you, I don't want to overdo it. You know, I don't want it to backfire and actually **DISCOURAGE** him. But today I broke down and said I'd go to the bookshop with David. He said if I'd finished the Camus, he could recommend something else. It was a tricky situation. If I said I'd finished *The Outsider* I'd have to tell him what I thought of it, but if I said I hadn't he'd think there was something wrong with me since it's not exactly **LONG**. But then **GENIUS** struck! I told him I'd finished it but was going to read it again, so I could fully appreciate all its subtleties. I said I didn't feel I could discuss it after just one reading. He seemed v impressed. No sooner did I hang up than Marcus rang. What was I doing, yadda yadda yadda? I said I was going to the bookshop, so he said he'd come too. Then it occurred to me that I could **EASILY** bump into Elvin in a bookshop, so I asked Disha if she wanted to come too. When we got there David was pretty quiet, but I reckoned that was because he was in literary mode (you should've seen the book he bought—it's thick as a brick!). Anyway, Marcus was in good form so we had some laughs. And we didn't meet Elvin.

My good mood evaporated almost as soon as I got in the flat. The MC was in my room **AGAIN**! This time she said she had a migraine (which might've had a shred of truth in it, since she didn't exactly look like a piece of art) and it was the only place she could lie down in *Privacy and Peace*. I said what about Justin's room; he hasn't sold his bed, has he? And listen to what she said!!! She said Justin needs **SPACE** because of his photography. And what about me?!! I'm an artist, or maybe a writer. I said how am I ever going to finish my story for the school magazine if I don't have any **PRIVACY AND PEACE**? And then you know what she said? She said J. K. Rowling wrote the first Harry Potter in a café so she didn't see what I was making such a fuss about!

SATURDAY 24 FEBRUARY

Is this injustice or what? Apparently, when Justin got his black eye he also lost his new camera. And is Justin being punished for this carelessness? Is he being treated like a pariah? Is he scorned and grumbled at and told **OVER AND OVER** how much things cost and how no one's ever going to buy him anything again? **NO, HE ISN'T!** He's been bought another camera! Sappho's right. There is no equality between men and women. Not in this house at least!!!

SUNDAY 25 FEBRUARY

Finally got around to hanging my wind chimes outside my bedroom window. They're absolutely brilliant! I lie on my bed, looking up at the glow-in-the-dark stars on the ceiling and listening to my chimes as though I'm camping in the Himalayas, watching the night sky and hearing the temple bells ringing in the distance. As someday, perhaps, I will!!! (Must check out what the scorpion situation is in the Himalayas before I go, though.)

MONDAY 26 FEBRUARY

A black star hangs over me! The curse of a whole coven of witches envelops me! You doubt that? Well, guess what's happened now! I'm the bold, innovative trendsetter who has her nose pierced and gets a dangerous infection as a result—and Catriona Hendley goes and gets a ring put through her lip like she invented body piercing! (You will notice that she did it **DURING HALF-TERM**— probably on the first day!!! That way, if it went septic and her lip swelled up like a zeppelin, no one would ever know. Talk about **deception and treachery**. I'm sure if William Shakespeare were to come back to life and run into

Catriona Hendley on the high street, he'd think she was Lady Macbeth in a short skirt and knee-high boots. "Gadzooks!" he'd cry. "You're back!") Everybody was hanging around talking about Catriona's lip before the bell. I told them about facial rings being a sign of slavery and oppression. I said I took my nose ring out as soon as I found out. Catriona said she reckoned lips rings were different. She said she wasn't really sure about kissing with it though. Someone said he'd be happy to help out if she wanted to practice, and everybody laughed, including David. He's obviously a better actor than you would have thought! It's good news about the kissing though. That should slow down her moves on Elvin a bit too.

TUESDAY 27 FEBRUARY

Disha had some **V DEPRESSING NEWS**. Elvin came by hers last night with Catriona Hendley! How could he do that? I feel as if someone's Rollerbladed across my heart. He knows Disha's my best friend! Did he think I wouldn't find out? That I wouldn't be excruciatingly hurt? That the *Hopes of My Love* wouldn't be dashed against the craggy rocks of Catriona Hendley's common good looks? Disha says it wasn't like they were holding hands or anything. He just brought her along because they're such **OLD** friends and he wanted to show her his award-winning documentary on cats, which (apparently) he left with Calum. I am not consoled. That's how these things start. One day they're joking around like brother and sister, and the next he's sticking his tongue down her throat.

WEDNESDAY 28 FEBRUARY

I think Justin must have a girlfriend because a girl called asking for "Just" (I was so surprised I said, "Just what?"), and when I asked him who it was, he said, "No one" (which is pretty ironclad proof if you ask me). The MC says I'm getting carried away by my vivid imagination (as usual!!!). She says this girl's probably just a friend. She says Justin has lots of female friends. Strange but true!!! Geek Boy's always had lots of girls hanging round him, but he's never gone out with any of them. I said I reckoned it must be time that changed. Why else was he nicking my underwear? And, anyway, as hard as it might be to believe that **ANYONE** from the human species could be interested in Justin, there was something in this girl's voice that sounded **POSSESSIVE**—and also suggested **SEX** (and if that isn't a thought to sober up every wild party in London, I don't know what is). I know from waiting at airports, etc., that some of the most unattractive people imaginable find partners (look no further than the parent Bandrys for proof!!!), so I think we have to accept that—though grossly improbable—it is not impossible that a female might be interested in my brother. She's probably a right tart.

FRIDAY 2 MARCH

Went to Disha's after school (again) hoping I might run into Elvin but he wasn't there. The good news was that Calum wasn't there either. I had another attack of genius. Maybe Calum had Elvin's phone number written down somewhere. Disha said looking in Calum's room for Elvin's number was a waste of time. (Was I mad? He's a **BOY**, for God's sake. Did I think he kept an address book?) But I was convinced it was worth a try. She was right about the address book, but Calum, being a Serious Filmmaker, does keep a notebook! It was in his desk. Elvin's number is written on the inside cover. Disha said it was too bad Calum didn't keep a diary. She'd give her red leather jacket (which, obviously, she **LOVES**) to read it. I said that even if Justin knew how to write, I wouldn't want to read his diary. I'd be afraid to. Knowing the superficial Justin Bandry is creepy enough without finding out his **deepest secrets**. Disha said yeah, but think of the v interesting bets we could make each other about what we would find in our brothers' diaries. Disha said she bet Calum is seeing an older woman. I bet her that Justin has boils on his bum. We laughed so much we thought we were going to gasp our last!

128

We found two other **V INTERESTING** things in Calum's desk: **DRUGS** (there was a lump of hash in a tin on top of his notebook) and **ELVIN'S MOVIE** (Purr Love—a film by Elvin A. Zagary). We debated what to do about the dope for about half a second, and then we decided that it should definitely be part of our intense, experience-seeking Dark Phase, so Disha hacked a bit off with Calum's Swiss Army knife and wrapped it up in a few of the Rizlas that were also in the tin. She hid it under the rug in her room for future use. Then we watched Elvin's movie. It really is about cats(!!!)—feral cats and the people who feed them. I have to say that I learned **A LOT** from it. You wouldn't believe how many people there are skulking around with carrier bags of cat food and bowls and stuff. D said she not only found it très depressing, but she also felt she now knew more than was necessary about the relationship between loneliness, madness, and felines. I, however, found it a disturbing but **V MOVING** and thought-provoking commentary on our times.

SATURDAY 3 MARCH

Awake half the night worrying about where I can hide my diary. I've been keeping it in my laundry basket, under my dirty clothes, but it doesn't seem very secure. (With her mood swings, the MC could suddenly decide to do the lot herself, never mind what she said about not being anybody's skivvy.) I don't know why I didn't think of it before. I mean, not only have I got the Mad Cow lying on my bed and snooping round when I'm not home, but I've got Justin bursting in whenever he feels like it to take pictures and nick my underwear and Nan wandering in when she forgets where the loo is. It's like King's Cross Station at rush hour. It goes without saying that **NONE** of these people respect my right to privacy. And also, in case you haven't noticed, Sigmund still hasn't got me my new door. Unless I rip up a floorboard, I can't think of any place that's **REALLY** safe to keep my diary. I have temporarily moved it to my closet, under a pile of stuffed toys. Even the MC doesn't go in there since the time she opened the door and was buried under an avalanche of clothes. (Well, where did she think I was going to put everything? If it would all hang in the closet, it wouldn't have been on the floor, would it?)

SUNDAY 4 MARCH

I DID IT!!! I rang up Elvin and asked him when he wanted to go for that bike ride. (Thank God he answered the phone. I've had just about enough of mothers! I'm not sure I could cope with another one, even if she is the woman who gave birth to such a remarkable son.) Elvin said we couldn't go today, because it's raining. So **NEXT SATURDAY**, weather permitting. I'm a little wary of trying a weather spell since obviously neither D nor I have enough *Peace and Privacy* in which to make one. Maybe I should get Nan to ask Jesus to make sure it's not pissing down.

Had a v intensive self-improvement day in preparation for next Saturday. I even read Sigmund's *Observer* so I'll know what's happening in the world if it comes up in conversation. (I reckon I don't actually need to read up on the cinema, even though it's Elvin's great passion, since I've been watching films from before I was born.) And also I bought a jazz CD (*Masters of Modern*), partly because jazz is the music of the intellectual and partly because it was v cheap. I even did **TWO** sessions of yoga! I felt absolutely brilliant afterwards, but nobody tells you that yoga makes you fart, do they? You wouldn't believe how much **NOISE** can come out of one body. How can people do it in a class? It must smell like any room Justin and Andrew have been in for more than five minutes. I reckon that's why they burn incense.

MONDAY 5 MARCH

Late for school this morning because I fell back to sleep when I was doing my yoga (lying dead still is v relaxing!) and the Mad Cow didn't wake me because she was busy! What sort of mother is so busy she forgets her own child?!! (What *am* I going to do if I **DO** turn into my mother? How will I ever live with myself?)

TUESDAY 6 MARCH

I'VE BEEN MUGGED! Can you even believe it?
I HAVE BEEN MUGGED! IN BROAD
DAYLIGHT!!! I hate to say it, but Nan's right. What
IS the world coming to? Here's what happened. I went
to see this bike that was advertised in *Loot* after school.
It's not exactly state of the art (it's white, pink, lilac, and
rust), but it was only twenty quid (which seems to me a
reasonable price for something you have to pedal). I took
the overground after I bought the bike because it was
MILES away and there was no way I was getting all
sweaty riding it home. I was talking to Disha on my
mobe as I came out of the train station. (Lila's NEVER
allowed to have another party because this time someone
threw up in the ficus. They'd covered it up with dead
leaves, but Mrs. Jenkins smelled it.) We were trying to
work out who the mysterious barfer might be. I had to
stop for a second to get my bearings, and then I went
left through the tunnel. That's when it happened. Two
boys were coming towards me, and I had to swerve a bit
to avoid running into them. The bike sort of wobbled,
and I was dealing with that (not easy with only one

hand!) when two more boys came up behind me. One grabbed my mobe and the other gave me a shove. I tore my best tights. The stripy ones Sappho gave me for my birthday. I was so traumatized by falling over with the bike and all that, I didn't even know my mobe was gone until I'd calmed down. No one came over to help me up or anything, of course (this is definitely the age of selfishness!!!). And the irony is that I could have been saved. David wanted to go to the library to work on our English project, but I said I couldn't. Well, I couldn't. I **HAVE** to have a bike by Saturday or I'm really going to have a problem. But if I could have that moment back, I'd make David come with me to see the bike. I'm sure he would've done it. He's very accommodating.

I must've caught her on one of her **UP** swings, because the Mad Cow was excruciatingly sympathetic about my mugging. She wanted to take me for an x-ray. And she wasn't even angry about me losing my phone. She just kept saying, "You poor thing. . . Are you sure you're all right?" over and over. Nan tried to cheer me up by reminding me that God Works in Mysterious Ways. Justin, of course, was his usual insensitive, uncaring self. He said I was the only person he knew who'd fallen off a bike without ever getting on it. I said at least I hadn't ridden in front of a police car. I wasn't as stupid as that.

Justin had three phone calls tonight—and they were **ALL FROM HER**!!! The Mad Cow answered the first time, I answered the second, and Nan answered the third. Nan has no shame, so she asked her what her name is. You won't believe this!!! It's Bethsheba!!! I knew she couldn't be **NORMAL** *and* interested in the Bandrys' other child. I usually spend some time before I fall asleep imagining all the brilliant things that are going to happen to me once I've left secondary school, but last night I spent it wondering what Bethsheba could possibly see in my brother. I know girls are different to boys. Boys see a short skirt and a big pair of tits and they go into meltdown. (I think it has something to do with male hormones, but Sappho says it's because men can see better than they can think.) Girls, however, are attracted by other things, like intelligence, talent, character, and personality. But Justin doesn't possess intelligence, talent, character, or personality any more than he possesses looks, for God's sake. I reckon Bethsheba either lost a bet or is a nymphomaniac with no standards whatsoever.

WEDNESDAY 7 MARCH

MEGA trouble at the Rancho Bandry!!! When I got home from school today the Mad Cow had a surprise for me. She'd decided to GIVE ME her mobe. She said she never used it, so she didn't see any reason why I shouldn't have hers. I tried to talk her out of it. I said I was pretty shaken from the attack and wasn't sure if I wanted to walk around with something that was so popular with thieves. As per usual, she paid ABSOLUTELY no attention to me. She said as long as I was careful and paid attention to where I was she'd actually feel better about me going out on my own if I had her phone. She went to get it. She was gone for eons. I crossed my fingers and sipped my tea. Maybe she'd totally forgotten where she'd put it. She hadn't. She returned in screaming mode. "Where's my phone? Did you take my phone? Did you go through my things? How would you like it if I went through your things?" (As if, right?!!) Yadda yadda yadda. I didn't break down though. I've been her daughter for sixteen years; I know how to do it. I just kept saying that I had no idea what she was talking about. What could she do? She's too lazy to dust for fingerprints. The whole time this was going on, Nan was sound asleep at the kitchen table. She only woke up when the MC started screaming that it was her phone I lost yesterday. "Tell the truth, Janet. It was my phone, wasn't it," she kept shrieking. "Trust in the Lord!" cried Nan. The Mad Cow said He was probably the only person in this house you could trust.

THURSDAY 8 MARCH

136

Disha, being of a v thorough (and, to be honest, less creative) nature, thinks it would be a good idea for me to try out my new bike **BEFORE** the weekend, but this seems a little reckless to me. I mean, what if I *do* get hit by a police car? (If you belong to a family like mine, you realize at a young age that you haven't exactly been born under a lucky star.) It would be bad enough if I had an accident *after* my ride with Elvin, but I don't want to be in traction when I should be with him. I reminded Disha that you never forget how to ride a bike, no matter how long it's been. That's a fact. She said she reckons it really is a fact, since her grandmother can't remember where she is most of the time, but last summer at the family barbecue she jumped on some child's bicycle and rode all over the garden, singing.

The MC was still up and in one of her anti–Mrs. Kennedy moods when I got back from baby-sitting tonight. She wanted to know where I'd been till nearly midnight, and I said across the road—where did she think I'd been? She said she thought Mrs. Kennedy, having children of her own, would realize that Thursday is a school night. Then she wanted to know if she was usually drunk when she came home in the middle of the night like this. Did she say where she'd been? Did she go out on her own or with friends? (I really think the MC must've played a v key role in the Spanish Inquisition in one of her previous lives.) I said so now you're Mrs. Kennedy's mother too. She said no, she's just my mother and that's hard enough. I pointed out that paranoia is also a symptom of the menopause, and she said not to forget that infanticide is too. I said it's lucky she doesn't have an infant then, and she said that's not what it means.

FRIDAY 9 MARCH

Marcus rang wanting to know if I fancied going to the cinema at the weekend. I said Disha and I were planning to see that Chinese film on Sunday and he could come along if he wanted. Then David rang with the same question, so I invited him to come along too. I consider this v fortuitous! It could be my chance to find out what's happening with him and Catriona.

Spent **HOURS** blacking in the stitching on my combats with a marker, as suggested by D. They are the absolutely only thing I have that's right for cycling on the heath (excruciatingly cool, but practical at the same time). And if I do say so myself, they look well wicked. I'm also wearing the bat top Disha gave me (partly because I **ADORE** it, and partly for luck). I doubt that I'll sleep much tonight, but at least my chimes will soothe my troubled, restless heart.

SATURDAY 10 MARCH

I'm writing this now, **BEFORE** my date with Elvin, even though I still have scads more to do to get ready. But as I finally drifted off to sleep last night, floating on the delicate sound of my chimes like a bamboo leaf on a warm spring breeze, it struck me that this could be a v momentous day. This may be the day I *Fall in Love* for the first time. (Which, as everyone knows, is the Most Important Day of Your Life!!!) If it is, then I will Never Be the Same Again. Think of it! I got up this morning and did the things I do every morning. I washed, dressed, and put on my makeup, as per usual. I had a cup of tea and a bowl of cereal, as per usual. Nan was arguing with her only son, Justin was stuffing his face while he read the paper, and the Mad Cow was talking to the radio. ("Yes," she was saying, "that's precisely what I think.") Everything normal. And all the time I didn't know I was about to *Fall Excruciatingly Madly in Love*. That while I was wiping up the juice that got spilled, My Destiny was brushing his teeth in Crouch End. So Wish Me Luck! The next time you hear from me I may be a woman in *L-o-v-e*.

SUNDAY 11 MARCH

I couldn't write last night, not after the day I had! And not because I am a woman in *L-o-v-e* (it's almost a miracle I'm not a woman in T-R-A-C-T-I-O-N). I feel like a Pawn of Fate. Delete all that crap about God loving me. Nothing in my life is easy. Nothing in my life goes the way it's meant to. (**HOLD EVERYTHING!** I have to get a cup of tea to calm my nerves before I put this excruciating tragedy down in purple and white. I'll be right back.)

I'm back! First of all, I should've known this wasn't going to be the Date of My Dreams from the moment I woke up and discovered that something had gone **RADICALLY WRONG** with my hair in the night. (I reckon there must be some cosmic law that says that the more important the occasion, the worse your hair is going to be.) Elvin said he'd meet me by the station in Hampstead. This ruined my plan of taking the tube. I didn't want him to see me coming out of the station, not after all our talk about how great it is to ride a bike, etc. On the other hand, there was no way I was riding up Haverstock Hill, even if I could have done it without bursting a lung. Not only did I not want to arrive for our first date all sweaty, but also I was a bit weak since I'd eaten **ALMOST NOTHING** since Friday night so I wouldn't feel too fat. Even walking, it's a bloody steep hill! I was beginning to think that they'd moved Hampstead (like to Finchley) by the time I finally got to the top. I was v happy to see that Elvin is a man of his word (I think reliability is important in a man). He was waiting outside the tube with his really flash bike (it made me wish I'd painted mine black and silver, but I thought it would impress him more if it looked really used). I got on before he spotted me and rode to the corner. He started laughing as soon as he saw me. Elvin said he hadn't seen a bike like mine in **EONS**. He said it looked like they'd reinvented the solid-steel frame. But he seemed impressed that I wasn't even out of breath. He said I was v fit and must have incredible thighs (Disha agrees that this was a v flirtatious remark).

The first forty-five minutes were **PERFECT**. We went to this little café before we actually started doing any strenuous exercise. I ordered herbal tea. (I felt pretty pleased with myself that I remembered.) Elvin ordered a double espresso. My tea tasted the way the water looks when you wash your knickers by hand, but it didn't matter because I felt about twenty. A sophisticated twenty. I reckon if you're a sophisticated twenty, you can put up with laundry water. Elvin told me some more about the film he wants to make. He wants it to show the side of life that you don't see in Hollywood movies. I said, "You mean, no guns?" and he laughed and said what a good sense of humor I have. It was all smiles and meaningful looks after that. We should've ended the date on minute forty-six, but we didn't. We went outside to get our bikes. Elvin explained the route we were taking (up there, first right, first right, first left—that sort of thing) and I nodded thoughtfully even though I hadn't a clue where we were going. (To tell you the truth, I've always found Oxford Street more interesting than Hampstead Heath. I mean, once you've seen a tree, you pretty much get the idea, don't you?) I watched Elvin take off. He was faster than the traffic. I got on my bike. I hadn't had any trouble riding the couple of meters to the corner the tube station's on (push down on the right pedal, push down on the left pedal, etc.), but for some reason this time I pushed left and pushed right and then I more or less fell over. (I reckon it was nerves because now I was with Elvin. Or sort of with Elvin. Elvin actually shot through a yellow light just before I tipped over. I thanked God. I didn't need any more of an audience than I had.) The next time I managed to stay upright. I was wobbling a bit, but I was also moving forward. Elvin was waiting on the other side of the lights, and as soon as he saw me he set off again. I couldn't go nearly as fast as he was going without being able to fly (I think he said his bike weighs about a pound), but at least I stopped wobbling. Everybody was right: You Never Forget How to Ride a Bike. Unfortunately there's another thing that's true, and that's that England never forgets how to rain. I was just sort of beginning to almost enjoy myself when it started to pour down. I rang my bell so Elvin would know I was having a good time (and also so he wouldn't forget I was there). He turned round and waved. And then he went right and disappeared. I went after him. I couldn't remember if I was meant to take the first left or the first right then, but he definitely wasn't ahead of me, so I went right, where there were more trees and less rain. It was the wrong choice. The only thing in front of me now was **DOWN**.

I don't think I'd ever seen such a v perpendicular hill before in my life! Aside from the fact that I was more hurtling than gliding down the hill, I wanted to stop before I went too far so I didn't have to walk back up. I touched my brakes. Absolutely **NOTHING** happened. I touched them again. If anything, I was picking up speed. This time I squeezed both brakes so hard I thought I was going to bend the handlebars. I started ringing my bell, but that didn't slow me down either. I closed my eyes and **REALLY** screamed. Elvin said I was lucky not to have broken anything. He said it was too bad my brother wasn't with me because he would've loved a photo of my face as I came down that hill (I made a mental note to tell Disha not to talk about my family to Elvin until I've had a chance to prepare him myself).

Being a gentleman, Elvin insisted on coming back with me to make sure I was all right. This was **FINE** with me. Sigmund had a group, the Mad Cow was out with Nan, and Justin's never home on a Saturday unless he's ill. My spirits rose even more when on the way home Elvin said that if I wanted, he'd come back next Saturday and fix my bike for me. I wasn't actually planning to ever get on the bike again, but I said that would be v kind of him and I'd even fix him lunch. He reminded me that I had my yoga class on Saturday afternoon (what a memory!). I said I'd changed it because Saturdays are just too busy.

And that's when all the good news stopped, because not only was Justin at home; he was watching a film on the little telly in the kitchen. Elvin immediately introduced himself and sat down. Following his practice of **ALWAYS HUMILIATING ME IF HE CAN,** Justin said, "Costello or Presley?" After I told him it was Elvin not Elvis and he should consider having his ears syringed, I went to change into something dry. And also do something about my hair and my makeup. But what did I see when I looked in the mirror? Not only was I soaking wet and slightly bruised (my hair looked even worse than it had when I woke up—I think I may cut it really short and dye it plum), but **MY FACE WAS STREAKED WITH BLACK!** I looked at my hands. They were black too. I looked down at my trousers. They were still black, but the stitching wasn't. Now it was gray. I even had ink on my legs!

By the time I got back to the kitchen, Elvin and the Abominable Brother weren't watching the film anymore;

they were talking about some photographic exhibition Justin's going to see next weekend! Really!!! As if anybody's interested. Trust my brother to be mute for most of his adolescence and then decide to make up for all those years of silence the first time I bring a potential boyfriend home. I put the kettle on. I suggested that Elvin and I could have our tea in my room, but Elvin said he was fine where he was. I drank my tea and watched the film while Justin tried to bore Elvin to death. I could feel depression descending, but I acted cheerful and normal. I don't want Elvin thinking I'm moody this early on. And also I have to consider my skin. My skin always erupts when I'm depressed—because of the stress. As soon as the film was over, Justin said he had stuff to do and left.

ALONE AT LAST! I wanted to cry out loud with joy! But not for long because then Elvin said he had stuff to do too and better shake a leg. As soon as Elvin left, I went to Justin's room to kill him, but he was already in his darkroom (that locks, of course!), so instead I went to Disha's for the night. (I used to wish that the Paskis would adopt me, but since the Night of the Fire Engines Mr. Paski's been more in the mood to have Disha adopted than take me on.) Disha said what happened with the ink was I didn't use a laundry marker; I just used a colored pen. It's all the Mad Cow's fault because we didn't have a laundry marker, did we? Sometimes I think she does these things on purpose.

Disha says she doesn't remember saying anything to Elvin about my brother taking pictures. She thinks Calum must have. I'm beginning to see some advantages to having a brother who doesn't speak.

MONDAY 12 MARCH

The Chinese film was well wicked! Neither I nor Disha really likes martial arts films (one time over at Nick's the boys were all watching a Bruce Lee movie and Disha and I talked through it because it was sooo cheesy and boring, and they told us to leave). Fight scenes are as tedious as car chases if you ask me. But this was different. This was more like a cross between Jane Austen and *Peter Pan* because there were two great love stories in it and the people could fly. And also the fighting was absolutely brilliant and not just the men, which, if you think about it, is still pretty unusual. The boys liked it too, even though it was a love story. There was, however, a bit of an incident. (Didn't I tell you nothing's ever easy?) The others went to find our seats while Marcus and I bought the snacks. It was a long queue, and we started messing around. I was trying to get my wallet from behind his back and I wound up pressed against his chest, but when we broke away most of my purple glitter bat was on Marcus! (Disha says maybe it's because it got so wet on Saturday.) It wouldn't come off Marcus though, would it? When we got back to the others Disha said it looked like we'd been snogging with a definite amount of *Passion*. Really! At the snack counter? And also I never got a chance to interrogate David about Catriona because he left right after the film for some reason.

TUESDAY 13 MARCH

I had to go to the library this afternoon because I got another notice about overdue books. I told the old bag I'd brought them back, and she said not those, the other ones. I said I didn't even remember taking that lot out, and she said one of the most astonishing things she's discovered in her hundred years as a school librarian is the high percentage of teenagers who suffer from amnesia. I said I'd look for them (the books, not the teenagers). When I got home the Mad Cow and Sappho were in session in the kitchen. There was one of those sudden meaningful silences when I shut the front door behind me. "Shhh! The child's home! Don't let her hear what we were saying about sex!"

Anyway, by the time I got to the kitchen they were going again at full volume, but now, of course, it wasn't about sex; it was about food. Simple as peasants, this lot. It's almost unbelievable. I shouted "Hi!" and they looked up, acting surprised to find me in the house. Sappho said hi back, but the MC gave me this sickly smile like she was trying to be brave and asked me if I'd had a good day. Needless to say, it wasn't a real question. Before I could even open my mouth to answer, they went back to banging on about root vegetables. Boring or what? I waited for someone to remember I was waiting to speak. It's just as well I wasn't holding my breath. "Did someone ask how my day was?" I asked loudly. "Well, to tell you the truth, it was pretty damn awful." Sappho reminded the Mad Cow that she was going to do her chart for her and said that maybe they should go somewhere quiet. This was a hint: they wanted me to vanish. I told them not to bother getting up; I was going to my room to commit suicide.

WEDNESDAY 14 MARCH

Disha got her period last night and didn't feel like coming
to school today (**HER** mother is v sympathetic about these
things, unlike some). I was on my way to see her this
afternoon when I bumped into David. He said he was
going to Camden to get his mother something for her
birthday, and I said if he wanted some feminine help I'd
be glad to tag along. He was excruciatingly grateful (even
when it isn't Christmas, boys hate shopping!!!). Now that
I finally had him alone, I didn't know how to start about
Catriona. Valentine's Day seems a long time ago. So we
talked about the film we saw on Sunday (which he didn't
seem to remember much), and school and stuff like that,
and then I said he seemed to be hanging out a lot with
Catriona Hendley lately—dead casual-like. He said,
"Really?" He said he's always hung out with her; he's
known her since they were six (she seems to have known
every attractive male in London since they were little—if
she wasn't so stupid you'd assume she must've planned it).
Then (v tellingly if you ask me) he quickly tried to change
the subject to how chummy Marcus and I seem to be
lately. Since I definitely don't want David thinking I'm
interested in Marcus (in case he says something to
Catriona, who says something to Elvin), I said we weren't

any chummier than usual, and I explained about the glitter. As I expected, he laughed v loudly, which I took as an admission that he'd had the wrong impression. It put him in such a good mood that he treated me to a coffee.

Naturally, the first thing I did when I finally reached the **House of Horror** was ring D. I said I reckoned we should set up in the matchmaking business, since David and Catriona are obviously on their way to being an **ITEM**. I mean, David denied it so much he might as well have admitted it. Disha, however, disagrees. She says I have no corroborating evidence. I think she's watching too many police dramas. Disha says Lila hasn't said anything about it, and we all know what a **BIG MOUTH** Lila has; there's no way she wouldn't at least drop a hint if things were hotting up between Catriona and David. And also Lila did say that they'd always hung out together, like David said. But I'm the child of a psychotherapist, and I believe in psychological evidence. Psychological evidence isn't based on what people say, but on what they might be saying.

FRIDAY 16 MARCH

Bethsheba rings at least twice every day, but tonight she rang **FIVE TIMES**! I was the one who had to answer the phone, because I was the only one home except Nan. I didn't want her to answer in case it was Elvin about tomorrow. I don't want him exposed to the darker side of my family life until we know each other better, say in a year or two. (You can bet your last Rolo that Catriona Hendley's grandmother isn't any more embarrassing than the rest of Catriona's incredibly perfect family. Catriona's grandmother isn't a Jesus freak; she's a baroness.)

Anyway, even though I told Bethsheba that Justin wasn't in and that I'd give him a message, she kept right on ringing. I finally unplugged the phone and went to take a bath. As per usual, the Mad Cow yelled at ME when she got home and realized the phone was disconnected. What if she'd been trying to get through? What if there'd been an emergency? I said what if she bought me a new mobe so she'd know that she could always get me if she had to, and she said what if I started ironing my own clothes and the moon turned blue?

You can see why people seeking enlightenment usually live in caves by themselves. (If it weren't for the lack of electricity and the snakes and scorpions I might consider it myself.) I really find coping with my family v draining. I hope I can survive long enough to get my own place. It's not easy to pursue a life that is intellectually stimulating as well as spiritually fulfilling in a house where everybody else is submerged in the **trivial** and the **mundane**. Mobile phones . . . the menopause . . . a little dye in the washing machine—what are these things compared to the great books, the great music, the great ideas? **NOTHING**, that's what. But how can I concentrate on *Higher Things* when I'm constantly being brought down to below ground level by the Bandrys?

SATURDAY 17 MARCH

MEGA DISAPPOINTMENT! Elvin rang this morning to say he can't fix my bike today after all. He said he was **REALLY SORRY** but he had to do something with his father that he couldn't get out of. I told him that, having unreasonable parents of my own, I understood. So I won't find out if we're destined to *Fall in Love* until next weekend.

To cheer myself up, I went over to Disha's. The other
Paskis were all out. Since I've got a **WHOLE WEEK**
before I see Elvin again I decided to use it constructively
and asked Disha to cut my hair—after all, the DP is a time
for experimentation. It took **EONS** because at first she
was so terrified of taking too much off that she hardly cut
it at all. Since Mr. and Mrs. Paski were out we then moved
into their room, where there are two **MAJOR** mirrors,
so I could monitor both front and back the whole time.
That worked pretty well until Disha got so obsessed with
making it **TOTALLY** even that she nearly exposed my
EARS (one of them is slightly imperfect). We called it
quits after that. I think it's too short, but Disha says it's
v trendy and immediate. (What else is she going to say?
That I look like my head's been mown?) We might've had
a fight, but then Disha remembered the dope we liberated
from Calum's desk. I pointed out that we didn't have any
tobacco, but Disha said she had a few fags stashed away.
I asked Disha when she started smoking, and she said she
didn't really smoke, she just liked to have one now and
then when she felt stressed, and she could stop anytime
she wanted. I said did she mean like Sigmund (who stops
at least twice a year) and we both laughed. We got some
snacks and put a film on, and then we got the hash out
from under the carpet. We weren't sure how much to use,
so we used the lot. I was trying v hard to follow the film,

so I didn't notice when Disha fell asleep. I didn't even notice that I **ATE ALL THE SNACKS** (a family bag of crisps, a family bag of tortilla chips, and an entire packet of custard creams) either. We both decided that this is not our drug. I definitely can't afford something that turns me into a human Hoover. I walked all the way home (the **REALLY LONG WAY**) because I reckoned I needed the exercise. Stopped off at the shops and bought some hair dye (*Purple Passion*).

SUNDAY 18 MARCH

Privacy being as rare as film stars in our house, I was v excited tonight to more or less have the entire flat to myself. Sigmund was out solving other people's problems, the Mad Cow was with Sappho, Justin had a date with Bethsheba (I know that's where he went because when I asked him where he was off to he told me to mind my own ****ing business. I wonder if I should tell this poor deluded—and possibly blind—girl that Justin wet the bed till he was ten before she gets too involved), and Nan was passed out in front of the telly (just for a change). I've had a couple of things I've been wanting to do that demand solitude. The first was to finally move my diary to a really secure location. Every day I put it somewhere different in my room, and I always stick a hair or a piece of thread between the pages so I'll know if someone's been reading it, but even though there's been no sign of tampering it makes me v nervous. I had such a premonition that the MC was trawling through my room on Friday, wanting to see what I'd written about her, that Ms. Staples asked me something twice before I realized she was talking to me. After class she pulled me aside to ask me if everything was all right because I seemed distracted lately. I told her it was because I was working on a story with a v good but complicated plot. She said she'd love to read it when it's finished. (I hope she forgets about it, or I may actually have to write something, which I'm MUCH too busy to do at the moment. No wonder Catriona sticks to poems. How long do they take?)

So anyway, I finally came up with the perfect hiding place. The garden! It's easily accessible, and since it's always raining no one ever really goes there. Even Sigmund's once-a-year barbecue extravaganza has been permanently postponed because last year he was so determined that the burgers were going to be totally cooked on the barbecue and not finished off in the kitchen, as per usual, that he set one of the deck chairs on fire. The other thing I wanted to do was DYE MY HAIR purple. I did the hair first because you have to leave it on for twenty minutes, so I could hide my diary while I waited. I went to the kitchen and got an empty flowerpot and a smaller pot with a plant in it. Then I wrapped my diary in a lot of plastic, put it in the empty flowerpot, and put the pot with the plant on top. Brilliant or what?!! It was raining, of course, so I stuck a carrier bag over my head so the dye wouldn't drip all over, then I nipped out and hid it in the shrubs. The wind banged the door shut behind me, but I didn't think anything of it. Not until I tried to get back in. That's when I remembered that it locks automatically. (What'd I tell you about being born under a curse? Of all the billions of families in the world, I had to be born to the one that puts a Yale lock on the garden door. It can't be an accident! There **HAS** to be a God. The only thing I don't understand is why He has it in for **ME**!) I couldn't exactly haul myself over the wall and go next door since all I was wearing was one of Sigmund's shirts and a carrier bag over my head, so I banged on the kitchen window and shouted. Sometimes I think if it wasn't for bad luck I wouldn't have any luck at all. The storm was making more noise than I was, and there was no way Nan would've heard me even if she'd been awake, not with the telly blaring away (not unless I was whispering something I didn't want her to hear). I felt like a ghost looking in at her old life, unseen and unheard. As the seconds turned to minutes, I saw my whole life shimmer before me in the steam from the kettle. Well, maybe not all of it, but **A LOT**. Mainly they were happy memories. I saw me and Disha walking in the rain in our frog wellies when we were little, and the beach that summer we went to Greece and the MC got sunburn poisoning (you should've seen her feet—they looked like she'd nicked them from a purple elephant). And also I saw all my friends' faces floating over the stove, smiling. And Elvin! I hadn't even tasted his sweet lips yet and now it would never be. But I thought to myself, well, if I have to die so tragically—before I even reach my prime—at least my last sight is a happy one!

Miraculously Nan shuffled into the kitchen before I died of **exposure and drowning**. Of course, then I had to sneak back out again to retrieve my diary since I had so much to tell. The MC wasn't the tiniest bit sympathetic or worried that I might have got pneumonia. All she was concerned about was what I was doing in the garden in the dark. I can see I'll have to keep my diary indoors after all. I can't keep popping in and out. Not when my mother has such a **suspicious nature**.

MONDAY 19 MARCH

The curse continues to work! When I woke up this morning I **SCREAMED OUT LOUD** when I saw myself in the mirror. I couldn't've been more **SHOCKED AND HORRIFIED** if I'd grown a second head. (Which is probably the only thing that could be worse than what has happened.) My hair has turned an **EXTREMELY** vivid magenta. I'm sure it's because of the hours I spent in the garden. There must've been a chemical reaction with something they're putting in the rain. The MC said it was

lucky I cut it so short or I might have blinded half of London. I tried not to let her negativity discourage me. I decided to make myself a **Dramatic Statement**. I dressed totally in black and wore my biggest silver earrings (**PERFECT** for the DP or what?!!). It's a shame my new boots fell apart like that, because they would've been the killer touch. Disha said I still looked v striking. David said he never realized I wore earrings before. Marcus said I reminded him of the girl in *The Matrix*, except that her hair wouldn't stop traffic.

The MC **ABSOLUTELY REFUSES** to believe that the Abominable Brother has a girlfriend. She reckons he would've told her if he really was going out with

Bethsheba. (I don't see why; he doesn't tell her anything else.) I said then why is she always ringing up like he's the talking clock and she doesn't own a watch? She said maybe Bethsheba hasn't realized that Justin isn't interested in her in *that* way. It's truly amazing that I haven't been permanently struck DUMB, living with these people. Like the girl's pursuing *Justin*? The MC really is losing touch with reality in a v frightening way.

TUESDAY 20 MARCH 159

Sappho asked how the vegetarianism was going, and I told her it was going well except I seemed to be gaining weight, not losing it like you'd expect. How can you put on weight when you're eating soya burgers, soya rashers, and chicken nuggets instead of hamburgers, bacon, and pork chops? It doesn't make sense. Sappho said, "McDonald's chicken nuggets?" She said there's twice as much fat per ounce in McNuggets as in a hamburger. I was shocked. I mean, it's chicken! How can you have fat in chicken? Sappho says it's chicken the way the Matterhorn at Disneyland is part of the Alps. She says that in America McDonald's chips have beef additives. She read all about it in some book. Sappho says you can't be too careful. Obviously not. It's incredible the things people don't tell you. They don't tell you there are Great Women Artists and they don't tell you there's all that fat in chicken. What else aren't they telling us? If you ask me, life should come with a book of instructions. D agrees. She says if you think about it, adults are **INCREDIBLY** irresponsible, not to mention they lie a lot—even to each other. We can't decide whether adults never had any principles, or if they lost them when they sold their souls for their mortgages and crap like that.

WEDNESDAY 21 MARCH

Disha wanted to know why I didn't go to the gallery with the guys last weekend. I asked her what gallery and what guys. She said some photographic gallery in the West End and Elvin and Justin. She overheard Calum and Elvin talking about it. I said she got it wrong. Justin went to some photographic exhibition on Saturday, but Elvin couldn't have gone because he had to do something with his father. Disha gave me her "oh yeah?" look. It's one of her more irritating habits. Like Elvin would dump me to go out with

Justin, right? What does she think? That they're **GAY**? And why would Elvin lie to me? It's not like we're even going out together yet, is it? I mean, Sigmund's always telling the MC untruths (e.g., last Sunday when he said he was doing something with his dependencies group, he wasn't because one of them rang up to find out if it'd been changed to Tuesday or Wednesday!!!), but they're married. You expect that sort of thing from people who have lived together long enough to feel suffocated.

THURSDAY 22 MARCH

Went for pizza with the usual suspects after school, except for Disha. I thought Disha'd given up on tennis, but she said she had a lesson tonight and wanted to go home and do her homework first. So it was up to me to watch for psychological **SIGNS** between David and the Hendley. And they were there! David and Catriona made sure they didn't stand next to each other or anything (in a v pointed, let's-act-like-we-hardly-know-each-other way!). At first the conversation was monopolized by Nick and Marcus in PlayStation mode, and then David started banging on about the pizza he makes at home. (I hadn't realized he's a New

Man. Justin, the Neanderthal, can barely microwave a croissant.) Marcus didn't find it too thrilling either. He started talking to me about some little art gallery near his place that he thought I should see. I wasn't **TOTALLY** listening because I was keeping watch to see if David and Catriona made eye contact. We had a v good time. Marcus did an impersonation of Bart Simpson accepting an Oscar that cracked us up so much we all had tears in our eyes.

I can't believe it! Turns out that the lesson Disha went to wasn't tennis—it was yoga. She said she'd heard me and Ms. Staples banging on about it so much that she got interested. And also she saw something on telly. I said if she was going to join a class, why hadn't she asked me to go too, and she said she had. She said I said I wasn't interested in a class because I had my book and it was cheaper. I don't remember this conversation **AT ALL!!!** Disha said, "And to think you're like this and you've only taken drugs the once. I thought you had to do it for a while before you lost your memory." I still think she's making it up.

SATURDAY 24 MARCH

The devil Nan's always going on about woke up this
morning in a really shitty mood and decided to give me a
small taste of what hell is like. First of all, I meant to get
up early because I had a lot to do before Elvin arrived
to fix my bike. I wanted to run through my yoga (so if
he asked me what I'd been doing, I could say my yoga).
I wanted to take a shower with the shower gel Sappho
also gave the Mad Cow for the winter solstice (so if he
noticed how good I smelled I could tell him I smelled
politically correct). And I reckoned it might be a good idea
if I didn't greet him in my pajamas so I needed to dress.
And also get everything ready for lunch. But I must've slept
through the alarm, because I didn't wake up till nearly ten.
It took me an hour just to find something to wear, so I
had to skip the yoga. Then when I opened the fridge I
discovered that the Mad Cow hadn't done a proper shop
yet. There was nothing to eat unless you liked bendy
carrots and mustard a lot. So then I had to change into
something I didn't mind sweating in and run to the shop. I
bought cheese, bread, tomatoes, and a large bag of crisps.
Toasted cheese sandwiches are my speciality. That and
peanut butter. As soon as I got home I changed again. I
was still looking for the sandwich toaster (microwaved just
isn't the same in my opinion) when the doorbell rang.

Elvin! Electricity shot through me. I had a big smile on my face and was already saying hello when I answered the door. The smile vanished. It wasn't Elvin. It was Bethsheba.

I was a bit taken aback. She wasn't at all what I was expecting. I was expecting someone rather pathetic who probably lives under a rock, but she was trendier looking than even Catriona Hendley. And v attractive in an emaciated art student sort of way. She wanted to know if Justin was in. I was too stressed to deal with her, and also if Justin was in his room, I didn't want him coming out while Elvin was here, so I said no. She wanted to know if I was sure. I said he'd left eons ago. Then she started screaming for him from the doorway. There wasn't any response, of course, so then she said to tell him she'd been by and that he should ring her. I went back to looking for the sandwich toaster. Justin strolled into the kitchen with his camera over his shoulder. I said I thought he'd gone out; didn't he hear Bethsheba SHRIEKING for him? He said who hadn't? He reckoned the whole road had heard her. He called her Bloody Bumshiva and said he wished she'd leave him alone, and I said why not tell her that instead of pretending not to be home, and he said what made me think he hadn't told her at least a hundred times? I said because he never tells anybody anything, and he said well, here was a first, then. I could tell Elvin that he couldn't wait for him because he had to go out. And as if this wasn't surprising enough (I mean, why would Elvin think Justin was going to wait for *him*? He was coming to see ME!!!), Justin then made a quick exit through the garden. I was watching him heave himself over the back wall when the phone rang. I picked it up because I thought it might be Elvin. It was Marcus, ringing to tell me not to eat lunch because we could get something after the gallery. I said what gallery? He said the gallery I'd made a date with him to see today because there are paintings in it that reminded him of my stuff. I acted all **shocked and horrified** (which I sort of was, though I was also too preoccupied with my date with Elvin to get **THAT** emotionally involved), and said I'd forgotten all about it. I said my nan had fallen again and we were all pretty upset and it had totally put it out of my mind. I said I couldn't go today because my parents were both out (true), and I had to look after my nan (would've been true if Nan were home). Marcus said well, what about next Saturday, and I said OK because the doorbell was ringing. This time it was Elvin (**FINALLY!**). I still hadn't found the sandwich toaster, but he said just a plain cheese sandwich would be great. (I like men who are flexible; I think that's another important quality to look for.) He wanted to know where Justin was and I told him he'd just climbed over the garden wall. I think he thought I was joking at first. I put the lunch stuff on the table and Elvin said he couldn't eat the cheese because it wasn't vegetarian. I said of course it was vegetarian; it was cheese. He said no, they weren't necessarily the same thing. He said cheese isn't vegetarian unless it has a green V or something on the packet to prove that it isn't made with animal glop. (And how was I meant to know a thing like that?) I said **OOPS**, I forgot. I haven't been a veggie that long. Elvin said vegetarians have to be really careful, and, so he didn't think I was **TOTALLY** clueless, I said it was worse for vegans because my aunt's a vegan and she reads the labels on **EVERYTHING** before she eats it, including salt. At last being related to Sappho has paid off!!! Elvin said he admires vegans. He said I had a v interesting family. Since this isn't true, and since even if it were true he wouldn't know it since he's only met Justin, I knew he was talking about me. I pretended to pick something off the floor in case I was blushing.

After lunch Elvin took a look at my bike, but even though he had a bag full of tools it turned out he didn't have the right one with him, so he said he'd come back next week. I thought maybe he'd suggest doing something else but he didn't. After Elvin left, I rang Marcus back, but he'd gone out. I decided to go to Disha's. When I got outside, Bethsheba was sitting on the step like that creepy bird in that Edgar Allan Poe poem. God knows how Geek Boy knew she'd be out there—perception isn't one of his strong points. I told her Justin wasn't back yet and she gave me this Mona Lisa smile and said she knew. Didn't I say someone who was interested in Justin had to be **REALLY STRANGE**?!!

SUNDAY 25 MARCH

Sappho and Mags rolled up unexpectedly tonight with a bottle of organic champagne. Sigmund (who is a **BIG FAN** of the grape) must've known somehow that there was going to be free wine on offer because he was actually home for a change. Psychologists aren't known for their sense of humor either, and Sigmund is no exception (unless it was marrying my mother), but he still tried to make a joke. "What's the occasion? You scalp another white man?" The Mad Cow, Sappho, and Mags all told him to shut up. Sappho said she had a major announcement. Turns out Sappho and Mags are pregnant! Well, one of them's pregnant (I think it's Sappho, but I got a little confused with all the shrieking this announcement caused).

Once things had settled down a bit, Justin decided to make a joke. He wanted to know if it was an immaculate conception. Instead of telling him to shut up the way they did Sigmund, Sappho said yes, and they all laughed hysterically (except for Nan, who said it was blasphemous and made her lips into a straight line). While they were laughing, Sigmund poured himself another glass of champagne (a big one). Then Nan decided she'd given them the silent treatment long enough and got back into the act. She couldn't understand how Sappho (probably) could be preggers when she's One of Them! Things weren't like this in *her* day. In her day people knew what they were meant to do, and if they didn't want to do it, they didn't make a big deal of it and have sperm injected into them. Sigmund told her not to start (which was pretty ridiculous, since she was already in full swing). Nan said she hoped they were going to have the baby baptized, the poor little thing. Sappho told her what she thought of that idea, and Nan stomped off to pray for everybody (she made sure she took her champagne with her though).

I hope Sappho isn't making a Big Mistake. I mean, she's only just started living with Mags. What if it doesn't work out? (It's never worked out before.) It seems like a pretty major step to take. Disha agrees. She says it's like marrying somebody on the first date. You'd think that someone who's been to university and is so politically sussed, like Sappho, would have a little more common sense, but Disha says that common sense is like the Canary Islands. There aren't any canaries left on the Canary Islands, and there's nothing common about common sense. Sometimes D can be v profound.

Sappho said I should've known about the cheese not being vegetarian because she'd told me often enough. She wanted to know if I ever listened to anything she said, and I said sometimes.

MONDAY 26 MARCH

It never ends, does it? What would everyone do if I weren't around to take the blame for everything? David was in a mood today because Disha and I didn't turn up for his pizza party on Saturday night. I said I didn't know about any pizza party. David said I did and that I said it sounded great when he invited everyone the other day. I don't consider some casual remark made when at least four other people are talking at the same time even close to a *real* invitation. Who could really hear him? And also he was going **ON AND ON** about pizza (it's bread, basically; there isn't *that* much to say), and he didn't make it excruciatingly clear that he meant **LAST** Saturday. Not to **ME**! I apologized abjectly and promised that even if Prince William invited me to a mega do at the palace on the same night I'd be at David's next pizza party. David was appeased. He said OK, it's a date. Next Saturday. Eight sharp. I wrote it on my hand, and later I made Disha write it down on paper so we don't forget.

Tonight when the phone rang Justin said that if it was Bumshiva I should tell her he wasn't home. I was **SHOCKED AND HORRIFIED** that he expected me to lie for him. He said he still had the negative of me sleeping with my mouth wide open and dribbling, and if I didn't want Elvin to see it I should just do what he said. I told him that was blackmail and it made him a criminal and he laughed.

TUESDAY 27 MARCH

It's a world of surprises, isn't it? Came home from school
to find the Mad Cow going through Sigmund's office. She
had a duster in her hand to make it look like she was
cleaning, but she was definitely turning it over. I told her
he didn't hide his cigarettes in his office, and she said she
wasn't looking for cigarettes; she was dusting. She said it
like she wouldn't care if he smoked himself into an iron
lung. (I'm not sure what an iron lung is, but it doesn't
sound good. I mean, it doesn't sound like something you'd
wish on the *Love of Your Life*, or even your husband.)
Maybe I'll never get married, if this is what happens. All
the *Passion and Romance* goes, and there's nothing left
to keep you together but the mortgage. I almost felt like
saying to her (woman to woman), "Jocelyn, don't you
remember how your blood used to race when you heard
his voice? How your skin tingled at his touch? How you
used to lie awake, imagining he was beside you? Where
did all that passion go?" But I didn't. If she ever did feel
like that (which does seem a bit unlikely) she'll have
TOTALLY forgotten by now.

D agrees that marriage sucks the romance out of a relationship. She says this is why Great Artists and Writers have traditionally been opposed to it. The *Soul* is always yearning to be free, and society's always trying to chain it down. Does that mean that the creative impulse is innately opposed to the needs of society? If man works on rules and the rest of the universe works on chaos, does society go against our **TRUE** nature? Questions, questions, questions!!! Sometimes I feel as if the Dark Phase may give me a permanent migraine. Watched some old *Friends* videos to calm my overworked mind. *Friends* I can understand.

WEDNESDAY 28 MARCH

HOT NEWS FLASH!!! Sara Dancer **DID IT**!!! She went to a party on Saturday and made it with some bloke from New Zealand. I said she'd been keeping pretty quiet about it, and Sara said that even though she definitely felt **LIKE A WOMAN** now there really wasn't that much to talk about. She said she'd had a few beers and didn't remember it all that well. I said I hoped she remembered using a condom and she said no. She said as a topic of conversation condoms hadn't exactly come up. (Just the penis did!!!)

THURSDAY 29 MARCH

Mrs. Kennedy said she wouldn't need me next week, but she wondered if I could mind the twins from Friday night to Sunday the weekend after next. At first I said no. I'm not totally sure about having the twins for long periods of daylight on my own. I'd have to do things with them and keep them entertained, which could be quite draining. And instinct told me that the Mad Cow would object. As you know, she's not v keen on Mrs. Kennedy, but she's even less keen on leaving me with ME on my own for a whole weekend—never mind with someone else's small children. Mrs. Kennedy said she only asked because her mum usually takes them when she needs a break, but she's gone to Australia. Mrs. Kennedy said it was a shame I couldn't do it because she was going to pay me double time, but she certainly wouldn't want to upset my mother after all my wonderful father's done for her. Double time! I don't like maths, but I do appreciate that it can come in v handy from time to time. A quick calculation told me that what Mrs. Kennedy was offering me was **FREEDOM AND PRIVACY** in the shape of a new mobe. So I threw caution to the wind and said I'd do it. I reckon the simplest thing is not to tell the MC. What she doesn't know can't stop me.

FRIDAY 30 MARCH

This afternoon Marcus said he hoped I hadn't forgotten that we're going to the gallery tomorrow. I said of course I hadn't. (It had **TOTALLY** gone out of my mind, which is understandable considering all the **STRESS** I've been under lately.) I told him I was really sorry but I still couldn't go, because of Nan's relapse and all. Marcus was v sympathetic (unlike anyone I'm related to). He wanted to know why Justin couldn't look after the old bag for a couple of hours and I said oh, come on now, you've met my brother; Justin's too selfish to do anything like that.

SATURDAY 31 MARCH

If Shakespeare's right and the *Course of True Love* is rougher than a trail up Mount Everest, then the feelings Elvin and I are going to experience (if we ever have ten

minutes alone) will be the *Truest Love* that's ever existed.
I am **THWARTED** at every turn.

First of all, the MC did another one of her vanishing acts
this morning without so much as a word to **ANYONE**.
God knows where she goes, but it definitely isn't
Sainsbury's since she's out **ALL DAY** and doesn't have
any food with her when she gets back. It was just as well I
shopped for lunch yesterday. This time I bought pasta,
pasta sauce with a big green V on it, and a bag of salad at
the health food store, so I felt pretty calm about that at
least. Nan was taking one of her afternoon naps, and
Sigmund, as per usual, was working his fingers to the bone
to pay my bills, so I was feeling **V POSITIVE**. But then
Justin Bandry, the boy who thinks home is where you
sleep, wouldn't leave the flat today no matter how much I
begged him. I was rushing round, trying to get ready for
Elvin, and Justin even made me check to see if Bumshiva
was "lying in wait" for him out front. (Melodramatic or
what? Men really are the most incredible prima donnas!!!)
She was. Justin said that in that case he wasn't going
anywhere unless there was a fire. (How **TEMPTING** is
that? If I wasn't afraid it might spread to mine, I'd torch
his room!) I said I didn't see why he couldn't go through
the garden, which is what he's been doing for **DAYS**, and

he said the man at the back booby-trapped his border so he can't land in it anymore. I told him that in that case he'd better stay in his room or I'd invite Bethsheba in for lunch. I reckoned that would keep Geek Boy out of the way. Which was just as well because the doorbell rang and it was Elvin.

The first thing Elvin said when I opened the door was had my hair always been this color? I said trust a filmmaker to be so observant. He obviously thought this was another example of my great sense of humor, so I laughed too. He wanted to know if Justin had gone over the garden wall again and I said no, he was in his room, but he was excruciatingly busy. Everything was V COZY after that. I got lunch ready while Elvin fixed my bike, just as if we were a real couple. When he was done he came into the kitchen, all triumphant. I said that was brilliant, cos now we could finish that bike ride, and he said sure but not today. Elvin read the label on the salad dressing while I drained the pasta. He couldn't eat that either, because it had anchovies in it. I was already thinking about how I was going to describe the afternoon to Disha, when Justin appeared, nose twitching (he's got the sense of smell of a police dog). I gave him every signal I could to make him go away (eyes, hands, eyebrows, mental telepathy—the lot), but except to ask when lunch was going to be ready he **TOTALLY** ignored me. I said should I be putting out four plates, and he gave me this big cheesy grin and said not to worry because Bumshiva had left. Elvin wanted to know who Bumshiva was. Justin started explaining that she was in a couple of his classes and had this fixation on him (ego or what?!!), and to my surprise Elvin not only didn't laugh at this piece of fantasy but acted all sympathetic. I was tempted to tell Justin what I'd like to do with his lunch, but I didn't want Elvin to see my harsher side just yet. Not until we've at least had our first kiss. So I put out three plates. And guess what? Disha was right about Elvin going to that exhibition last weekend, because that's all they talked about while they shoveled my lunch into *their* gobs. As soon as they'd finished eating, Justin asked Elvin if he wanted to see what he was working on in his darkroom. As sweetly and meaningfully as possible, I told Justin that Elvin had come over to fix my bike, not look at his pictures. And what did Elvin say? Elvin said he'd already fixed the bike and he'd **LOVE** to see Justin's pictures. (If Justin shows Elvin even **ONE** of me—even if I look a stone lighter than I really am and am **MIND-BOGGLINGLY GORGEOUS** in it—I swear I'm going to destroy his bloody darkroom.) I know Elvin was only being polite. He probably thinks he has to be nice to my brother even though he's the biggest pain in the bum that ever lived, but I was so **ENRAGED** I had to force myself to remain pleasant. As soon as I heard Justin's door close, I raced outside to see if maybe Bethsheba had come back, but (**NATURALLY!!!**) she hadn't. Just wait till the next time she calls round. We'll see who lies for Geek Boy then. Rang Marcus, but he'd gone out, so I'm going over to Disha's. I don't trust myself to be alone with my brother.

SUNDAY 1 APRIL

Disha, Marcus, Nick, Siranee, and I all turned up at David's at eight o'clock last night, as requested. David opened the door, and then he sort of stood there, half smiling at us as if he thought he was on *Candid Camera* or something. The boys were hungry, as per usual, so they sort of barged in and the rest of us followed. David said something about checking the dough and dragged me into the kitchen with him. I've never seen him so angry. Not even the time he got thrown into the biology pond in his white suit. He wanted to know if this was some sort of April Fools' joke or something. I said, "Um, duh, you invited us over for pizza, remember? I even wrote it down!" David said he was under the impression that he only invited *me* over for pizza. I said, "Really?" He said really. He said now we were going to have to order more pizzas and I could pay for them, which was pretty unreasonable if you ask me. David said he thought it was more unreasonable to invite four people to dinner at someone else's house without bothering to tell him. I told him to look on the funny side. I mean, considering the fact that out of the lot of us David and I are the only two who speak English as our first language, it's pretty ironic that we can't seem to communicate. David said I'm the one who can't communicate.

MONDAY 2 APRIL

I'm still pretty irked by what happened with Elvin on Saturday. I know it's all Justin's fault, but I can't help thinking that Elvin could have shown a little more interest in ME. Disha thinks I may be misinterpreting things. She says maybe by ignoring me he was showing how interested he really is. Disha thinks Elvin feels so comfortable with me that he doesn't think he has to make any special effort and just acts normal. Like we've been seeing each other for eons. But what about *Passion and Romance*? That's what I want to know. I mean, I know lunch for three isn't the same as a candlelit dinner, but he could at least've talked to me a bit!!! Because I was so **HURT AND DISAPPOINTED** I decided to ask Marcus if he wanted to go to that gallery after school one day this week. Marcus said the exhibition was over. He said it like it was my fault.

TUESDAY 3 APRIL

Will I ever find peace from the slings and arrows of Outrageous Fortune? (It's beginning to look like the answer to that question is **NO**!!!) Between school, Elvin, David, Marcus, my family, and trying to keep my sanity and sense of humor despite all of them, I found it v difficult to get to sleep last night. It was raining pretty hard, so even the wind chimes weren't as soothing as usual. I never count sheep (I don't know about anyone else, but I can never get the sheep to jump over the fence), but eventually I was so desperate that I started going through my multiplication tables. I reckoned that should do it, since it's usually only with **SUPERHUMAN** effort that I manage to stay awake in maths. I was soaring through the fives when I heard someone outside. At first I thought it was a cat. Then it made another noise, and I knew that if it was a cat, it wasn't your average sort of cat; it was more like a

PUMA. I was at the window in a flash! There was just enough light from the other flats for me to make out a **dark sinister figure** crouched like a v large puma on the garden wall. All those lectures from the MC about what to do in an emergency finally paid off. I quickly squeezed through my door, raced into the kitchen, and dialed 999. Then I went to wake up Justin. (He's always had more of a sense of adventure than the parents, and he acts without thinking.) Justin wasn't asleep; he was working on some project for college at his desk. He grabbed his camera and ran to the kitchen. I grabbed his heaviest tripod and followed. The rest, as they say, is history. Justin was just stepping out of the garden door with a tea tray over his head when I got to the kitchen. He shouted something threatening like "Don't move!" and then he started snapping. I reckon it was the first flash that caused the intruder to fall off the wall. I ran into the garden brandishing the tripod and warning him that the police were on their way. Justin yelled at me to be careful of his tripod, and the dark sinister figure roared, "For @#$%'s sake, Janet, are you trying to kill me?" It was Mr. Burl. My wind chimes were driving him **BONKERS** and he'd hauled himself up on the wall to try and cut them down. He stabbed himself in the calf with his pocketknife when he fell off the wall.

WEDNESDAY 4 APRIL

Everybody at school was v impressed by the way I tackled
Mr. Burl last night. And also they thought it was the
funniest story they'd ever heard. Not so at home, though.
Sigmund was **APPALLED** by the behavior of both of his
children. He said no wonder Justin's always being injured
in the line of duty. I no longer even try to make any sense
out of what these people say, but I did mutter oh right,
my brother the law enforcer. Sigmund said he meant
taking pictures. Like that black eye. Somebody decked him
for taking his photo. **GET THIS!!!** Apparently the
Abominable Brother is sort of famous for taking photos of
street people (although they don't always appreciate it).
He's even had his work in some gallery. (You really would
think **SOMEONE** would tell *me*, wouldn't you?!!) All
this time I thought Justin was just really clumsy. And as for
me, Sigmund couldn't decide if I was just incredibly stupid
or if I'm criminally insane as well. The Mad Cow thinks I
should offer to walk Mr. Burl's dog for a week to show
him how sorry I am. The police, on the other hand, said I
did the right thing and that Mr. Burl had no business
skulking around in the dark like that, and I'm with them.

The only one who's shown any pride in my quick thinking and resourcefulness is Nan. She said it was what she would've done. She said next time to wake her up too.

THURSDAY 5 APRIL

The stress just doesn't end! I was just selecting my supper (vegetarian stir-fry dinner or pasta with salmon) when Disha rang in a **PANIC**! Elvin turned up, looking for Calum, but Calum was out and Elvin decided that rather than wait around with Mr. and Mrs. Paski, he'd walk her to our yoga class. I said what yoga class, and she said the one I told him we go to together. What a memory! It's lucky Elvin fixed the bloody bike, that's all I can say. I told Disha to walk **SLOWLY** and I raced to the yoga center. I'd already put my mat at the back when they arrived. I acted well surprised to see them. And then, as if I wasn't under enough stress already, Elvin decided to stay for the class to see if it was as great as we said. We started out with some breathing (easy), and chanting (dumb but easy), and then even though it was almost night we Greeted the Sun (not too hard and vaguely familiar). All was well until we had to stand on one leg and stretch out our other limbs. Well, we're not flamingos, are we? I lost my balance and Greeted the Floor. Mary, the instructor, said she didn't think my lip was cut as badly as the amount of blood gushing from it would make you believe. You'd think I'd deserve a quiet night after that, but God wasn't through with me yet. I had an encounter with the law on the way home. A motorcycle cop pulled me over for not having lights on my bike! Sappho's right—they should use taxpayers' money to hunt down criminals.

184   FRIDAY 6 APRIL

Ms. Staples wanted to know if I'd finished that story I was working on, since she was hoping to read it over the Easter break. I said not yet. I said I was trying to do some v complex things with plot and style, which was holding me up a bit. I said I was aiming to finish it over Easter, when I had more free time. She said she can't wait.

Came straight home to pack for my secret weekend across the road. Nan and Justin were sitting on the sofa. Geek Boy doesn't usually have any expressions except asleep and awake, but today he actually looked **WORRIED**. In the kitchen the MC and Sigmund were reenacting the war in Kosovo. I asked what was happening. Justin said Sigmund had just informed the MC that he had a conference to go to this weekend and had only come home to get his kit and the MC went **BALLISTIC**. Nan said that even though Sigmund's her son she wouldn't blame my mother if she beat him to death with his electronic organizer. (Spoken like a true Christian, right?!!) I said that personally I couldn't see what she was all wound up about since he was never home anyway. Justin found another expression—contempt—and said he reckoned that was the whole point. Even baby-sitting the twins has got to be less stressful than dealing with this lot!!!

SUNDAY 8 APRIL

I think it was that Scottish poet Robert Burns who said that no matter how well a mouse or a man plans things, they don't always turn out the way they were meant to. He speaks for me. I planned the weekend carefully and pretty flawlessly. I told the Mad Cow that Disha's parents had invited me to their cottage for the weekend (no phone!). She didn't put up any objection. After Sigmund skulked off on Friday and the smoke cleared, I kissed her and Nan goodbye and walked out of the front door with my satchel over my shoulder.

The twins and I spent Friday night alone. It wasn't too bad, because Mrs. Kennedy left a lorryload of food for us and the twins were watching videos in their room anyway, so I spent most of the night on the phone. Disha (heavily disguised just in case she bumped into my mother on the street) came over on Saturday morning. It was just as well Disha was there, because the twins are definitely more active in daylight. They wanted to go outside (which, of course, was OUT OF THE QUESTION), so we had to work v hard to keep them occupied. We were both EXHAUSTED by lunchtime. And then the doorbell rang. Disha looked at me and I looked at her. I told her not to answer it, in case it was my mother (you never can tell, right?). The doorbell rang again. DEMANDINGLY. Paying no attention to anyone else, as per usual, the twins ran out of the flat to answer it. Just in case it was the Mad Cow, I tried to work out a plausible excuse for being at Mrs. Kennedy's and not in Wales as I raced after them.

The good news was that it wasn't my mother. By the time I got down the stairs, the twins had opened the front door to a pair of policemen. It's amazing how policemen always look like policemen, even when they're not in uniform, isn't it? All I could think of was now what have I done? Shane was shrieking that his mum wasn't home. The policeman wanted to know if his dad was in. They weren't after me! I nearly collapsed with relief. "He's in jail," I said from the stairs. The policeman said, "Not anymore, he's not." Can you believe it? Mr. Kennedy's escaped! Once I'd made it clear that neither Mr. nor Mrs. Kennedy was home, more policemen materialized. They couldn't believe I didn't know where Mrs. Kennedy was, so I explained that I hadn't expected a raid, had I? But I did have a phone number. The Mad Cow was so **SURPRISED** when I arrived home with Disha, the twins, and approximately half the police force of north London that she didn't make a big deal that Disha and I weren't in the countryside. After the police left, the MC said she thought she should call Mrs. Kennedy too, so she'd know the boys were all right and all. So I gave her the list of emergency numbers Mrs. Kennedy'd left. She stared at it for a few seconds, and then she went over to the memo board and stared at the number Sigmund had left for a few seconds, and then she said maybe I should ring; she was going to take a bath. She was in there for ages. Disha thinks I should **REALLY** consider a career in literature, no matter what Ms. Staples thinks of my plots, because you just can't make this stuff up.

Acting **TOTALLY** out of character (and much to my amazement), the MC said she wasn't going to boil me in oil or anything like that for lying to her about going to

Mrs. Kennedy's. She said that in future she'd appreciate it if I made some vague attempt to tell her the truth, but all in all she thought that compared to some people I hadn't actually done anything wrong. And also I'd coped pretty well with the cops and all, and at least I was trying to earn money to buy a phone and wasn't nicking cars or doing drugs or worse (whatever she thinks **WORSE** could be!!!).

MONDAY 9 APRIL

LISTEN TO THIS!!! The police think Mr. Kennedy escaped because he found out Mrs. Kennedy is fooling around with another man!!! Is that **DRAMA** or what? It's like something out of a Quentin Tarantino movie, except so far dozens of people haven't been brutally murdered. Just in case, though, the cops have Mrs. Kennedy and the twins in hiding till they get Mr. Kennedy back. Sigmund got home well late last night, after everything had pretty much simmered down. He was v upset to hear what had happened, though he didn't hear it from the MC since she's even angrier with him now than she was on Friday and not only refuses to speak to him but has moved back into her bedroom with Nan!!! Sigmund wanted to know if the police had considered the possibility of Mr. Kennedy coming after **HIM**, since he's been trying to help Mrs. Kennedy sort out her life. The Mad Cow happened to be within earshot and said the only words she'd spoken to him since he got home, which were that it *had* occurred to her, and she only hoped that Mr. Kennedy was a really good shot. The menopause is giving her a v black sense of humor.

Since it's the Easter holidays and all, and since he seems to have forgotten that we never really finished our bike ride, and since I'm **ABSOLUTELY** desperate for something to do, I rang Elvin and suggested that we pick up where we left off. He said he'd love to. He'd **REALLY, REALLY** love to. But he hurt his hand doing wing fu or chung ku or whatever it is he does, so he's incapacitated at the moment. He'll ring me as soon as the swelling goes down. At last I have something to smile about.

TUESDAY 10 APRIL

Not only is the tension between Sigmund and the MC **GINORMOUS,** but Sigmund's acting even more peculiar than usual. For months we've hardly seen him because he's always working, but now he's canceled

EVERYTHING and refuses to leave the house. I asked the MC what she thought was wrong with him and she said (AND I QUOTE!!!), "He's a total jerk, that's what's wrong with him." I WAS SHOCKED. Really. It's one thing me slagging him off—after all, being critical of your parents is part of the teenage experience, isn't it? But Jocelyn's married to him. Also, she's my mother. I don't think it can be healthy for a child to have one parent telling her what a total waste of space and air her other parent is. It feels like it breaks some really major rule. People on the same team are meant to be loyal to one another, aren't they?

Most of my mates have gone away for the Easter holidays (including Disha, whose parents were lent a cottage in France for a few days and decided to go at the last minute). So since I'm well BORED (there is no phone in the French cottage and D was forced to leave her mobe at home) and feeling very STRESSED by the war between the Bandrys, I decided to forgive David for the pizza incident (time really is the great healer, isn't it?) and asked him if he wanted to spend the day with me. He wanted to know who else I'd invited along, and I said no one. We went bowling up Finsbury Park. I told David all about Mrs. Kennedy and the police and everything. He could hardly stop laughing.

WEDNESDAY 11 APRIL

Rang up Sara Dancer to see if she wanted to hang out,
but I never got a chance. **SIT DOWN AND GRASP
THIS!!!** Sara Dancer thinks she's **PREGNANT**!!! Her
period's **DAYS** late. I said don't be ridiculous; you can't
get pregnant from just **ONE** time, and Sara wanted to
know what I was doing during sex education—having one
of my out-of-body experiences? I said but **THE FIRST
TIME?** That really does seem a bit harsh. Sara said it's not
like learning to skate or something like that; you don't
need a few tries before your body gets the hang of it. I
asked her what she's going to do and she said get a
pregnancy test, so, since I had nothing better to do
anyway, I went with her to buy it. She insisted on going
somewhere where it would be **IMPOSSIBLE** for us to
bump into anyone who knows either of her parents, which
largely left us with the options of Mayfair and Stoke
Newington. Mayfair's easier to get to. I am très happy that
I'm not the one who needs a pregnancy test, but I have to
say that the whole experience made me feel v grown up—
like a heroine in some depressing realistic novel. We got
a bit lost coming back and ended up caught in all the
tourists wandering round in confusion outside the V&A
with their cameras and their guidebooks. Sara and I were
discussing the fact that we haven't been in the V&A since

primary school when I suddenly noticed a familiar face in the middle of a clutch of Japanese tourists who were having their picture taken on the steps of the museum! "Good God," I cried, "there's my brother." Sara wanted to know who his dishy friend was. I said what dishy friend and she said the one taking everybody's picture. CLAMP YOUR MOUTH OVER YOUR DENTURES!!! It was Elvin! He was holding the camera with TWO HANDS!!! Which suggests that either he's made a MIRACULOUS RECOVERY or he was LYING TO ME!!! I told Sara I didn't know who he was. I was MUCH TOO STUNNED to speak!!!

I decided to have a few words with the Abominable Brother tonight. I asked him what he thought he was doing, hanging out at the V&A with Elvin, who, after all, is meant to be MY friend. Justin wanted to know if there was something about him that attracted insane women or if we were all insane.

I've been thinking A LOT about Sara Dancer. I decided that at our age pregnancy is a bit like death. You never really think it's going to happen to YOU!!! And also although I'm sure there must be TONS of Great (or even just excruciatingly good) Women Artists and Writers who have also been terrific mothers, I couldn't think of any offhand, so I flipped through you, dear diary, to see if I could find any. I couldn't. As an experienced child minder, I know how demanding and time-consuming even children who don't need their nappies changed can be. When would you have time to **CREATE** if you had a baby? How could you devote yourself to your work if you were tied to the schedule of an infant? Sara Dancer wants to be a fashion designer not an artist, but I reckon it's not **THAT** different. You still need *Peace and Quiet* to get your ideas and all. Plus fashion designers have to go to lots of shows and celebrity parties and stuff like that, which is hard to do if you're breast-feeding.

THURSDAY 12 APRIL

I can't tell you how relieved I was this morning when Sara rang to say the test was negative. She sounded pretty relieved too. She said if she'd known it was going to be negative, she would've bought some condoms while we were in the chemist's.

I was just getting ready to settle down to writing my story when Marcus rang to say he's returned to Ye Olde London. He asked me to go to the Tate Modern with him, so I said

I'd been dying to go but somehow had never got round to it. It was all right. The building's pretty cool. But Marcus and I agreed that even though we're *Young and v Avant-garde* we're not really into modern art. Marcus says *Soul* has been replaced by mere cleverness. I was v impressed. I thought that was a v profound perception and said so. Marcus said what did I think, that he was just another extraordinarily handsome face, and I said no, I never thought that. (Sometimes we really crack each other up!!!) We got v bored of **soulless art** in a very short time, so we went out for coffee. I told Marcus all about Mrs. Kennedy and the police, of course, and he laughed even more than David had.

To show you exactly how **TENSE** the atmosphere is at home and how desperate we all are for some neutral conversation, Justin actually asked me how I liked the Tate Modern at supper. I said I thought some of it was pretty cool, but that on the whole I felt that modern art had replaced soul with mere cleverness. Justin said he'd read that piece in the *Guardian* too.

SATURDAY 14 APRIL

Nan's all wound up because she read in the paper that according to some poll nearly 50 percent of the population has no idea why we celebrate Easter. I said I thought it had something to do with the founding of Cadbury. Both Justin and the MC laughed, which is pretty much a first for one of MY jokes. Nan said she just hoped I *was* joking.

EASTER DAY

Instead of the Easter Bunny, the Easter Bethsheba turned up at the door with a v peculiar-looking hard-boiled egg for my brother. She said she made it herself. I said it looked like it'd been cooked in tea and she said it was, in Darjeeling. Then she wanted to know if Just was back from Greece yet. (So THAT explains why she hasn't been haunting our road lately!!!) It took me a few seconds to absorb this. I was about to say oh yes, he's back and he's sitting in the kitchen right now, when Nan suddenly loomed up behind me and shouted right in my ear that something had gone wrong with Justin's flight and we had no idea **WHEN** he was getting back. Bethsheba said oh, but before she could say anything else Nan shut the door very firmly in her face. I said to Nan that I was **SHOCKED** that she'd lied like that. I said is that what Jesus would've done? Nan said no, of course He wouldn't. Jesus would've zapped Bethsheba like a fig tree or turned her into salt.

The MC said that so we could all eat the same thing she was declaring Easter a no-meat holiday and she made fish. You'd think that even Sigmund could carve salmon without too much trouble, but you'd be wrong. He was just about to make the first cut when a car backfired in the street. He hit the floor as though he'd been shot. Everybody thought it was **HILARIOUS**, except Sigmund, who said it was obvious none of us read the papers or we'd realize just how violent a society we live in.

MONDAY 16 APRIL

There was some jubilation in the Rancho Bandry tonight because Nan's finally gone home. Sigmund was so excited that he actually volunteered to drive her, but the MC said she was going out anyway and she'd take her. Sigmund said what about supper, and the MC said that she reckoned a fifty-five-year-old man with three psychology degrees should be able to manage supper on his own. Fortunately I don't have to sit around half the night while Sigmund tries to find the pasta because Disha's finally back and I'm going over there. I feel like someone being released from prison. Or a bird released from its cage. It wouldn't've been so bad if I could at least have talked to her on the phone. God knows how anyone survived before the telephone was invented. I may have to name my firstborn Bell.

TUESDAY 17 APRIL

I can't tell you how good it was to see D!!! I feel like I've been living in the **wilderness** without her. Thank God there was no one home when I got back. I don't think I could **BEAR** to interact with my family right now. It's only after finally talking to someone who understands me and thinks and feels as I do that I realize what a strain I've been under this past week.

Life really is full of **SURPRISES,** isn't it? Hang on to your wig—**YOU'RE NOT GOING TO BELIEVE WHAT'S HAPPENED NOW!!!**

After I filled you in on recent events, I started working on some sketches for art. (I wish I'd gone to see those paintings with Marcus. Which of my styles is it?) Anyway, I got pretty immersed in that. (Art is all-consuming, after all.) I heard Justin come home (he was yelling at someone—presumably Bethsheba—to leave him alone), and then I heard Sigmund come in (he was singing some old song). Next time I looked up it was nearly seven. I was famished. I went to the kitchen to see how long it was till supper. Sigmund was sitting at the table, drinking a glass of wine and smoking a cigarette and staring into space. I asked him if he was planning to feed us anytime tonight. He told me to get the take-away menus. "Where's Mum?" I asked. He said didn't I get the letter she left me in my room? I said I hadn't seen any letter, but I went to look just to keep him happy. I reckon I must've been in what Sigmund calls denial, because it didn't even occur to me that the MC had abandoned ship (well, it wouldn't, would it?). I suppose what I vaguely reckoned was that she must've taken a sudden holiday. After all, it's a well-known fact that middle-aged women who are sick of their boring lives often go on holiday to Greece and have affairs with gigolos, waiters, or fishermen. (It's almost romantic in a depressing sort of way.) And also menopausal women are known to be impulsive and unpredictable too. The letter was on top of my chest of drawers, under some stuff I'd decided not to wear. She hasn't gone to Greece. She's gone to Hackney to stay with Sappho and Mags!!! You could've knocked me down with a paper clip. **REALLY!!!** The first time I read it, I thought it was a joke until I got to the end and realized there wasn't any punch line. The second time I read it, I didn't know what to think. It might as well have been written in code for all the sense it made. Then, obviously unsettled by this unexpected and shocking news, I made an **UNPRECEDENTED** move!!!

I showed my letter to Justin. He had one too, though he didn't seem as shocked and surprised as you'd think. The letters are pretty much the same. They both say that the Mad Cow's sorry to leave us like this, but she's been feeling very unhappy and confused lately, and having Nan around was too much added stress, so she's decided she needs a break. She'd be thrilled if we wanted to call her, but she can understand if we're angry and upset and don't want to speak to her just yet. She said if Justin and I were younger she wouldn't have gone, but we're old enough now to be able to get on without her for a while. I said to Justin, "I don't get it. She didn't need to leave to get away from Nan. Nan's gone back to Clapham." Justin said she didn't leave because of Nan; she left because Sigmund's such a jerk. I said but he's always been a jerk, and Justin said, "Wake up, Janet. The man Mrs. Kennedy's been cheating with is dear old Dad." I was so gobsmacked I didn't know what to say.

Right after the take-away Justin sloped off as usual and Sigmund, clutching his wine and muttering about how the MC could at least have left him the car, staggered off to the Bunker. I don't know if they thought I was going to clean up the mess from supper, but if they did they were **REALLY** deluded. As soon as I was alone I rang D to tell her what'd happened. As one would expect, Disha was **SHOCKED AND HORRIFIED**. She said imagine Mrs. Kennedy (who looks like she was invented for **SEX**) having it off with Sigmund (who looks like he was invented to wear old clothes)!!! And also D said she'd always thought of my mother as being so **STABLE** and family-oriented. And what day was that? Disha said no really. Who did I think kept everything together? Sigmund can't even find the coffee without help. And then D remembered that she had said the MC seemed tense, which is true. I said I still reckoned that leaving me with Sigmund and the Abominable Brother is **V DRASTIC**. D said at least I have to admit I have an interesting life. She says if I don't become a major novelist I should consider writing for the soaps!!!

WEDNESDAY 18 APRIL

At first I was v calm and philosophical about the MC
leaving home. And, anyway, I was pretty shocked by
Sigmund's behavior—you expect more from a
psychotherapist, especially if he's your father. But D and
I have already discussed how everyone has a secret self,
so I wasn't totally unprepared. In reality we are on our
own in this life and have to learn to deal with that and be
independent and responsible. (That's one of the really good
things about being in the DP: you're not looking at the
world through the rose-tinted glasses of a child. You
appreciate how **deep and painful** life can be.) I could tell from
my reaction that the last few months have **REALLY**
matured me. But tonight I was left alone in the kitchen
with the dirty dishes (**AGAIN**) and it finally hit me what
the MC's done!!! She's **ABANDONED ME**!!! Me, her
only daughter!!! If you ask me, she might as well've left
me in a skip with a note pinned to my nappy on the day
I was born. In fact, it would've been a **KINDNESS**!!! At
least it would've saved me all those years of
DELUSION—of thinking I was wanted, cared for, and
loved! I mean, what does it matter what she wrote in her
letter? She didn't give one nanosecond's thought to how
this would **AFFECT ME**!!! If that's not **MEGA
SELFISH** I don't know what is. I burst into tears. I just

sat there at the table, surrounded by the empty containers of fast food, weeping like an orphan, my *Soul* howling. **HOW COULD SHE DO THIS TO ME?** Eventually I pulled myself together. After all, I am adult enough to accept the fact that I am **ON MY OWN**.

THURSDAY 19 APRIL

I'm going to get a T-shirt made that says **Home Is Hell**. When I got up this morning, not only were all the dirty dishes, etc., exactly where they were last night, but Sigmund was still in the Bunker playing Bob Dylan at a volume more appropriate to dance music. Loyal friend that she is, D came round to console me. She wanted to tidy up, but I said I reckoned Sigmund should do it, since it's his fault the MC left. Neither of us could stand the **doom and gloom** or Dylan for long, so we arranged to meet Marcus and David for lunch so I could get my mind off my woes. That didn't exactly happen, since my woes were mainly what we talked about. David and Marcus were well shocked about Sigmund and also about the MC's behavior. They agreed with me that though leaving home is pretty typical for **MEN**, mothers aren't meant to do things like that. If you ask me, it's unnatural for a mother to just walk out on her children without even a little warning. I can understand her abandoning Justin—if you ask me, she waited eighteen years more than she should have—but I'm her **DAUGHTER**. How could she do this to me? Neither Marcus nor David knows the answer to that question. (The only one who disagrees is Disha, who is showing some feminist tendencies heretofore unsuspected. D says she reckons the mistake the Mad Cow made was in not tarring and feathering Sigmund before she left!!!)

Anyway, we had a v interesting discussion about marriage over lunch. I said the thing that really got me was how **SUDDEN** this all was. I mean, my parents argued a lot, but they *always* argued a lot, especially lately, so how was I meant to know it was different this time? That's what married couples do, isn't it? They argue. Everybody agreed. Marcus said his parents once had a four-day argument over the right way to boil an egg, and David said his mother once threw a Weight Watchers chicken dinner at his dad, straight from the microwave. Even Disha agreed that though the government's always telling everybody that they should be married, it's probably a lot less stressful to join an army in combat.

FRIDAY 20 APRIL

Despite the fact that he never spoke to her when she was
here, Geek Boy rang the MC tonight, probably to tell her
that we're running out of food and there's no washing
powder left. (Sigmund, as per usual, was in the Bunker.
He seems to be going through all five hundred Bob Dylan
albums in chronological order, which means he won't be
out till the weekend at the earliest!!!) After he finished
grunting into the phone, Justin said the MC wanted
to talk to me, but I said to tell her I was busy. In an
UNPRECEDENTED gesture of sensitivity and
diplomacy, Justin put the phone on hold and said I should
talk to her or I'd hurt her feelings. I said what was he
trying to do, make me cry? What about MY feelings?
Then he said I was acting like a child!!! Is that rich or
what? I said I wasn't the one who ran away from home.

I'd LITERALLY just hung up from talking to D when
the phone rang again. I practically jumped!!! It was Sappho.
She said the MC was really hurt that I wouldn't talk to her.
I said she wasn't the only one who was hurt. How did she
think I felt? Sappho said maybe I should try to put myself
in the MC's place, and I said that was not a location I ever
wanted to be in.

As you know, I was v traumatized when I saw Elvin at the V&A with my parents' other child. But I have had time to think about it and I realize I may have overreacted. Just because Elvin didn't **LOOK** as if he were in pain doesn't mean that he wasn't. Riding a bike and holding a camera aren't exactly the same thing, are they? And maybe he was suffering when I spoke to him on the phone, but his hand started to heal rather spectacularly after that. So I decided to put it behind us, and after I talked to D I rang up Elvin. As a Serious Filmmaker (and an older man) I reckoned he might have some valuable advice for me during these difficult times. His mother said he wasn't in. I said could she tell him Janet rang. She said Janet who? I said Bandry. And do you know what she said?!! She wanted to know if I was Justin's sister!!! Maybe I should encourage Geek Boy to visit India for a couple of years. He'd love India. It's absolutely **FILLED** with poor people who live on the street.

I couldn't get to sleep so finally I decided to see if Sigmund had left any wine in the fridge. I reckoned a glass of wine would help me relax. It was one in the morning, but the light was still on in the Bunker. At first I thought Sigmund had thoughtfully turned his stereo down really low, but then I realized the sound I could hear was him talking on the phone so I tiptoed down the hall to listen. I reckoned he was talking to Mrs. Kennedy. He wasn't. He was talking to Mrs. Bandry!!! Even more **AMAZING,** he was begging her to come home. I can only assume it's the car he's after.

Everybody was going to David's tonight to watch videos, but I stayed home. When you have a major upheaval in your life (like your female parent running away and your father having it off with a neighbor), it makes you **introspective and reflective**. Not for me the bright lights of Hollywood and the innocent chitchat of my friends over snacks and fizzy drinks. The crisps would have turned to ashes in my mouth. My mood demanded the comforting glow of candles, the warm scent of sandalwood, and anguished jazz squeezed from the *Soul,* the notes flowing through the night like blood.

SUNDAY 22 APRIL

Sigmund has emerged!!! He doesn't look great, but at least he's turned off the stereo and he says he's going to go back to work tomorrow. Apparently Mr. Kennedy's been apprehended. I said did this mean Mrs. Kennedy was back and I'd be baby-sitting the twins on Thursday, and Sigmund just shook his head v slowly but didn't say anything. I'm taking that as a no.

Bethsheba was back in her usual position on the front steps when I got home from D's this afternoon. Since I'd more or less forgotten about her, I was v surprised. She said she'd been trying to ring Justin for days, but the phone was always engaged so she decided to come over in person. I said she should ring him on his mobe because there were other people in the flat besides Justin who also needed to use the phone. I said anyway, I was under the impression that they'd broken up, and she said no, it was just a misunderstanding. She said I must know how difficult Justin can be. **TELL ME ABOUT IT!!!** I told her if she was waiting for Justin to get home she was going to have a long wait because he'd gone round to our aunt's. She wanted to know where Sappho lived and I told her. If you ask me, it serves Justin right. If he spent more time with his own friends he wouldn't be spending time with **MINE**!!!

If somebody doesn't do the dishes soon not only are we going to run out of plates and cutlery—we won't even be able to have a cup of tea!!!

I was watching telly tonight to take my mind off all my problems. (I don't believe one can be a **TOTAL INTELLECTUAL** all of the time; there are times in life when simple amusement is necessary, which I reckon explains why so many Great Writers and Artists are also alcoholics.) I must've sat on the remote because suddenly the set switched itself on standby. That was when I realized that Sigmund was on the phone in the Bunker again. Stealthy as a cat, I moved towards his door. This time I was **ABSOLUTELY** sure he was talking to Mrs. Kennedy because he kept saying the L-word. And then I heard him say my mother's name. I couldn't make out what else he said, but at a guess it was probably that he thought there was someone outside the door because he suddenly yanked it open. I said I was looking for my earring and he believed me.

MONDAY 23 APRIL

Justin threw a major wobbly when he got home this afternoon. He marched into my room without even knocking. I said excuse me, but you can't just barge into a person's room like that, and he went **DEEP** red and started shaking like a Chihuahua. Then he started screaming!!! (He's always been v volatile and emotionally unstable, but if he keeps this up he'll have a heart attack before he gets out of art school.) He wanted to know what was wrong with **ME**!!! I said **ME**? What did I do? He said I was the **MORON** who told Bumshiva where he was yesterday. Was I **OBLIVIOUS**? Or did I really live on my own planet? Didn't I see that Bumshiva's a mad, deluded creature who's been stalking him? It was just as well I was already lying on my bed or I would've collapsed from laughter. If you ask me, the Abominable Brother's been watching too many movies. Stalking! I mean, really, get a life. It's pretty obvious that the girl isn't working with a complete deck or she wouldn't be interested in Justin in the first place, but **STALKING**?!! People who stalk aren't trendy art students; they're usually balding losers with bad dress sense and worse breath. Justin said it wasn't funny. He spent the night at Sappho's because even though he told Bethsheba to go away she stayed outside the house and he didn't want to end up trying to get home from Hackney with her in the dead of night. I said I was under the impression that he and Bethsheba were back together, which was why I told her where he was, and he asked me who told me that. I said well, who did he think? He said I was a con man's dream. Wait till he finds out I gave her his mobile number.

Disha says it's possible that Bethsheba really is stalking Justin. She says she thinks certain sorts of stalking can happen to anyone, like measles or something. She says you'd have to have an **obsessive personality,** but artists often do. I said give me a **BREAK**. Who could get obsessive about a boy who shops in Oxfam and always smells of developer? Disha said apparently Bethsheba.

TUESDAY 24 APRIL

Nan rang last night to find out why no one's rung her to see if she's all right. Since the only person who would think to ring her isn't here anymore, I admitted that the MC had run away from home. Nan said she always knew something like this would happen, right from the moment Sigmund turned up at the church in a wedding coat and high-tops. She offered to come back and look after us. Personally this struck me as a reasonable idea, since Nan believes in Victorian values like meals and household maintenance, but Sigmund looked like this was all the good news he needed for the rest of his life and lied and said we were doing just fine on our own—he's not **INCOMPETENT,** is he? (I couldn't hear Nan's answer, but even though she's old she isn't exactly stupid!) Then he said it wasn't as if the MC'd left for good; she was just taking a leave of absence. I just hope the MC knows that.

WEDNESDAY 25 APRIL

There are some disadvantages to being a motherless child that I haven't thought of before. For one thing, there's the food. I'm the first to admit that the MC's one of the worst cooks to ever make lumpy gravy, but at least she does cook. Now that she's living it up in Hackney, nobody can be bothered to go shopping, so we're still living on take-away. (Take-away's all right for a couple of days, but you'd be **AMAZED** how quickly the charm wears off. I mean, it's not what you'd want as a steady diet. Especially not when your choice is pretty much pizza or pizza if you don't want to do the dishes.) So, since no one's shopping, we're not only out of food, but stuff like detergent and bog rolls as well (we're reduced to using newspaper—I can't tell you how **GROSS** that is). And also I had a report to type up for history, and even though Sigmund can type almost as well as the MC he **REFUSED** to do it for me. It took me **EONS** with only two fingers! The other thing is that the health and sanitation standards of the flat have slipped so much that it's getting v hard to find things, and if you put something down you have to check first that you're not putting it in something disgusting. I said to Sigmund, didn't he think it was time he found the Hoover, and he said why didn't I find it? (Yeah, right! If he thinks I'm going to be his SKIVVY he can think again.) I hope he is right and the MC will come back once she's calmed down or I may have to move to Hackney too!!! I don't think I could survive indefinitely with Sigmund in charge.

Disha says to look on the bright side. I asked her what that is. Disha says that this is meant to be our year of spiritual and intellectual growth, and I'm definitely doing that. And also it's pretty dark. I said that if I get stuck living on my own with Sigmund for the rest of my life it's going to be more like a black hole than a Dark Phase. But I can see she has a point.

THURSDAY 26 APRIL

I told Disha how selfish I think the MC is being, and she said have I thought about how I'd feel if I were in the MC's place? I said she was beginning to sound like Sappho, and she said no REALLY. What would I do if I found out

my husband was running around with another woman—
cook him supper? I said not likely. If I cooked him supper
it would only be to dump it over his head. D said
EXACTLY!!! She said if I'm going to be pissed off with
anyone, it should be Sigmund.

FRIDAY 27 APRIL

Disha's got a point. Sigmund's always telling me **I'VE** got
a long way to go before I'm an adult, but if you ask me so
has he. He doesn't **DO** anything! He just goes to work and
then he comes home and goes back to the Bunker to listen
to **Mr. Doom and Gloom**. (I should've dumped all his Dylan
albums in the bin while he was out.)

I decided to break down and ring the MC tonight. It's
ironic considering how she drives me crazy, but I'm really
starting to miss her. And besides the general quality of life
descending quickly into Third World levels, I don't know
where my PE kit is and I got yelled at again by Mrs. Wist
today. The MC sounded surprised to hear from me. I said I
wasn't angry with her (which is more or less true, though
I'm still v irked). I said I'd been thinking about it and if
I'd found out my husband was running around with

another woman I would've gone too. And then I asked her when she was coming back. She said, "For God's sake, Janet, I've only just left." I said no, really. I said if she didn't want to live with Sigmund anymore (and who could blame her?), wouldn't it make more sense to make him move out? The MC laughed, but not AT me (for a change!), more like in surprise. She said my Dark Phase must really be changing me because I'm actually sounding more mature. If you ask me, it's the MC who's changing (I've ALWAYS been v mature for my age), but I didn't say that to her. I said it's a well-known fact that children of divorce grow up suddenly (I heard it on *Oprah*).

SATURDAY 28 APRIL

Disha was hauled away for the weekend by her parents, and the usual suspects (David and Marcus) are doing something male and juvenile together tonight, so I sat myself down and went into *Creative Mode*. It's true what the poets say about it being a REALLY rotten wind that doesn't blow some good somewhere, isn't it? With the exception of people like Tolkien and Jeffrey Archer, lots of writers use their own lives for the basis of fiction, but up till now I'd always felt that my life wasn't BIG enough for that yet. But after what D said about not being able to make up the stuff that happens to me, I decided to give it a try. It's about a girl whose self-centered father uses her to mind his lover's children while they go to cheap hotels, and then the lover's psychotic husband breaks out of prison to avenge himself on the self-centered father, but when the girl captures the psychotic prisoner and becomes a hero, her mother finds out what's been going on and leaves home. I'm calling it "Reasons Never to Get Married."

SUNDAY 29 APRIL

There wasn't any milk in the flat this morning, so I had to go out and get some. **AGAIN**. I'm going to start keeping a record. Anyway, it's not even eight in the morning and the first thing I see when I step outside is the **girlfriend from hell**! Since I got all that grief from Justin for just talking to Bethsheba, I decided to ignore her. She called my name, but I kept right on walking. When I got back with the milk she v. as standing in front of our door. I told her Justin was still sleeping, and she said how nice it would be if she could have a cup of tea while she waited. I told her there was a café nearby. She didn't budge. I said would she mind stepping aside so I could get into my own home, and she started crying and going on about how she LOVED Justin and how if only she could talk to him they could patch everything up. (Talk about drama queen!!!) Not only was I DYING for a cup of tea, but I was going to have to dig a cup out of the sink and wash it before I could have one, so I was less than MEGA sympathetic. I told her that as far as I could see, Justin had even less interest in her than he did in translating Mansfield Park into Sanskrit. I advised her to get a life.

That's when she went for me! (Literally!!!) I know this may sound naive, but I really wasn't expecting to be attacked on my own doorstep. Which gave Bethsheba the advantage. She lunged straight at me and knocked me over. (If you ask me, it's a miracle I wasn't wounded.) It's just as well Sigmund's a light sleeper. He charged out in nothing but his boxers (which is not a pretty sight—if photographs of Sigmund in his boxers were given out in sex ed there'd be a whole lot less pregnant teenagers in this country, believe me), shouting like a kung fu warrior. Of course, it wasn't **Satan's spawn** he was shrieking at. It was ME—the innocent victim!!! What the hell are you doing? Yadda yadda yadda . . . What I was actually doing, besides trying to push the stupid cow off me, was open the milk so I could try to drown her. Sigmund got us both inside and then he went to wake up Justin, but Justin had already escaped through the garden despite the booby traps. Sigmund, of course, was **TOTALLY** oblivious to what had been going on, but Bethsheba was excruciatingly happy to fill him in. Anyway, Sigmund was all Mr. Concerned Parent and Comforting Shrink, while I (of course!!!) got stuck with making the tea and washing out **THREE** cups, etc.

Eventually Bethsheba calmed down enough to say she was sorry for trying to cut my promising life short, but she was in a v emotional state (um, duh . . . really???) and she couldn't believe I told her to **GET A LIFE** when that was what she had. Neither Sigmund nor I knew what she was on about. We looked at each other, and then we looked at her again and Sigmund said, "Pardon? I'm not certain I understand—" and Bethsheba started crying again. **HANG ON HARD TO ANYTHING THAT ISN'T CEMENTED DOWN!!!** Bethsheba, through a churning ocean of tears, said that what she meant was that she's carrying Justin's child! Even Sigmund didn't have an answer for that one. He just sat there like a beached fish, staring at her. I took advantage of this moment of **SHOCK AND HORROR** to pretend I had to go to the loo (not that either of them noticed). I walked straight out of the front door and went to Disha's. (What would I do **WITHOUT HER**? I ask you!!!) D called it the Attack of the Killer Cow. She said did I really think Justin would be stupid enough to get Bumshiva knocked up and I asked her if she'd met my brother. I was going to stay over at D's, but in the end I decided to come home and work on my story. It's so **ABSOLUTELY** true that suffering fuels creativity, isn't it? Let's face it: shallow, happy people write Burger King jingles, but deep, unhappy people write *War and Peace*.

218   MONDAY 30 APRIL

Justin stayed at Sappho's again last night and the Mad Cow brought him home this afternoon. She said she reckoned it was time the four of us sat down and had a **SERIOUS** talk. Sigmund said too bloody right and immediately started going on about Justin being a disgrace. The MC wanted to know what he was on about, and when Sigmund explained she and Justin both fell about laughing, which made Sigmund go into morally superior mode (which is probably his favorite). He said he was shocked that the MC, of all people, would condone Justin's irresponsible behavior. Justin stopped laughing long enough to say that he wasn't like Sigmund and didn't indulge in irresponsible behavior. Sigmund said that getting your girlfriend pregnant and then dumping her like a hot potato was pretty irresponsible in his book. Justin said first of all Bumshiva'd **NEVER** been his girlfriend and that second of all she **WASN'T PREGNANT**; she was just insane. Sigmund said, "That's what you say." Justin said it was. The Mad Cow had already heard the whole tortured tale from Justin (obviously), and she **TOTALLY** believed him. Sigmund got all haughty and raised an eyebrow and all like he'd completely forgotten he was meant to be trying to encourage the MC to like him again and said **REALLY**? The MC said **REALLY**. She said if Bethsheba actually was preggers it was either an immaculate conception or the father was someone we didn't know. Sigmund asked her how she could be so sure, and the MC said because Justin wasn't a compulsive liar like the only other male in this family!!! I just sat there, observing all of this like a Great Writer would, but I have to admit I was v impressed by my mother. I'd never seen her like this before. Then she said that anyway, Bethsheba's histrionics weren't what we had to talk about. You could tell from the way he immediately started nodding and looking v serious like someone on *Newsnight* that Sigmund thought this meant she was ready to come home for good. But I was watching the **NEW** Jocelyn Bandry and I had my doubts (and also I noticed she didn't have a suitcase with her). You should've seen Sigmund's face when the MC said she was coming home, but only because he was moving **OUT**. (If he doesn't stop looking like a dying fish I may have to change his name to Trout!!!) Sigmund wanted to know where this brilliant idea came from but the MC just smiled and gave me a look.

TUESDAY 1 MAY

I gave Ms. Staples my story today. It's over **TEN PAGES**. Ms. Staples said no wonder it took me so long to write. I said I **KNOW** how busy she is and all (apparently teachers, like whales, are an endangered species!!!), but I would **REALLY** appreciate it if she could read it as soon as she has a chance. Now that my creativity has been turned on, it needs **FEEDBACK**. Ms. Staples said she'd do her best.

WEDNESDAY 2 MAY

I'd like to think that the new Jocelyn Bandry owes something to me and the Dark Phase. I mean, it's possible, isn't it? She saw me struggling to live deeply and meaningfully and she was inspired. She looked at her own life and she saw its **shallowness and triviality,** and she was finally ready to face the pain and remake herself. The Dark Phase has **DEFINITELY** affected Disha. I have always known that I will never have a better friend than Disha Paski—not if I live to be a **MILLION** (though, really, who would want to?)—but now she has surpassed herself. How? I hear you ask. And this is how. To stop my torment Disha took direct action. She just came right out and asked Calum if Elvin was interested in me or not. Calum said or not. Disha said she was wondering because Elvin had sort of made a play for me, and Calum said, "Oh, that." D wanted to know oh what. Turns out Elvin was hoping that if he got friendly with me he could get Justin to help him with his film. My only consolation is that Elvin's stupid film is also the reason he was cooing round Catriona. Because of her father. He was hoping he could get it on telly. I'm **DEVASTATED**! Mine is a trusting nature. I can't believe someone could be so duplicitous. Disha says well, live and learn—that's what life's all about, isn't it? (She really has **MATURED**!!!)

THURSDAY 3 MAY

NOTHING lasts for ever, that's the truth. Last week I was a motherless child, and now I'm a fatherless one. Sigmund moved out tonight, although, as Justin says, it isn't as if he's gone FAR. He's got a flat in Kentish Town. The MC's saying this is a trial separation, but Sigmund couldn't have been halfway up the road before she was rearranging their bedroom. Already the living standards have risen. There's bog roll in the bathroom and we had meatballs and spaghetti for supper. It wasn't as bad as I remember, but that could just be because I've been on the Sigmund Bandry Starvation Diet. Now that Elvin has proved not to be a Man of Principles but a **Snake in the Grass of Love,** I've started eating meat again. I mean, really, why not?

David rang tonight to see if I wanted to go to a film on Saturday night. I said yes. He said just you and me, right? I said of course. At least I know that David is an honest person and interested in ME—not my brother. And also (since I'm not COMMITTED to anyone yet) I've already arranged to go ice-skating on Sunday with Marcus.

FRIDAY 4 MAY

I AM DEFINITELY ON MY CREATIVE WAY!!!
Ms. Staples was v impressed with my story. She says it's
funny, insightful, and ORIGINAL. She even wants to
publish it in the school magazine. She did say we'll have
to sit down and discuss it IN DEPTH, of course. She
says she still feels I have a problem with implausible plots.

223

I said it's not MY problem—it's LIFE'S.

GLOSSARY

999 U.K. equivalent of 911

A-LEVEL MATHS Advanced-level exam in mathematics, usually taken at age 18

A–Z street map of London

BANGING ON (colloq.) talking endlessly

BISCUITS cookies

BLOKES (colloq.) men/boys

BLOODY (colloq., vulgar) very; used as an all-purpose intensifier

BLOODY-MINDED (colloq., vulgar) stubborn, pigheaded

BOG ROLL (colloq.) toilet paper

BOXING DAY the day after Christmas

BRILLIANT very good, excellent

CAPITAL GOLD British radio station; plays oldy-moldies from the sixties

CARRIER BAG plastic shopping bag

CHEMIST pharmacy

CHIPS french fries

CHUFFED (colloq.) pleased

COW PAT pile of cow dung

CRISP, CRISP WRAPPER potato chip; bag of potato chips

CROUCH END a neighborhood in north London

CUPBOARD closet

DINNER LADY a woman who cooks or serves food in a school cafeteria

DISHY (colloq.) very good-looking; cute

DRIBBLING drooling

DWEEBLE (colloq.) made-up word meaning geek, idiot

EASTENDERS popular soap opera set in London's East End

FAGS (colloq.) cigarettes

FANCYING (colloq.) having a crush on

FIT (colloq.) good-looking, attractive

FIVER five-pound note

FLASH (colloq.) flashy, glitzy

FLAT apartment

FROG WELLIES rubber boots with frog faces on them

GARDEN backyard

GCSEs General Certificate of Secondary Education exams, usually taken at age 16

GET OUT borrow or take out, as a library book or video

GINORMOUS (colloq.) made-up word; amalgamation of *gigantic* and *enormous*; very big

GIVE A TOSS (colloq., vulgar) care

GOBS (colloq., vulgar) mouths

GOBSMACKED (colloq., vulgar) astounded

GONE OFF gone bad; spoiled

HALF-TERM one-week midsemester vacation

HAVING IT OFF (colloq., vulgar) having sex

HEATH, HAMPSTEAD HEATH big park in
    north London

HERS, HIS, MINE, OURS (colloq.) her place, his
    place, my place, our place

HIGH STREET Main Street; the main road in a town

HOLIDAY, HOLIDAYS vacation

HOTTING UP becoming more intense

JELLY Jell-O

JUMPER sweater

KIT clothes and/or equipment assembled for a
    specific purpose

KNICKERS underpants

LOO (colloq.) toilet, lavatory

LOOT British magazines and web service advertising
    used goods for sale

LORRYLOAD (colloq.) truckload; a large quantity

MARKS & SPENCER British department store;
    a "family" store, the kind of place your mum
    drags you to for "back-to-school" clothes

MATES (colloq.) friends

MI5 the United Kingdom's security intelligence agency

MINCE ground beef

MIND babysit

MOBE (abbr.) mobile (cell) phone

NAFF (colloq.) cheesy, tacky

NAPPIES diapers

NEWS AGENT'S small shop selling newspapers, candy, cigarettes, and such

NEWSNIGHT current affairs program on British television

NICKED (colloq.) stole

NIPPED OUT stepped out

OVERGROUND above-ground trains

OXFAM charitable organization based in the U.K.; runs shops selling third-world-produced and secondhand goods

PE KIT clothes worn for Phys. Ed.

PHONE BOX phone booth

PISSING DOWN (colloq., vulgar) raining heavily

PLASTICINE a soft modeling material

POUND basic monetary unit of the United Kingdom

PUDDING dessert

PUSHCHAIRS strollers

QUEUE (verb) stand in line

QUID (colloq.) pound

RASHERS thin strips of meat, especially bacon
(in this case soya)

RIZLAS brand name for cigarette papers

ROUNDED ON (colloq.) turned on; started attacking
verbally

ROW, ROWING argument, arguing

SAATCHI GALLERY contemporary art gallery in
London

SAINSBURY'S large U.K. supermarket chain

SARKY (colloq.) sarcastic

SAS (abbr.) Special Air Service

SERVIETTE napkin

SIXTH FORM YEARS last two years of school
before university, equivalent to twelfth and
thirteenth grades

SKIP Dumpster

SKIVVY (colloq.) servant

SLAGGING OFF (colloq., vulgar) insulting,
deriding, criticizing

SNOGGING (colloq.) kissing passionately

SNOOKER a variety of the game of pool

SODS (colloq., vulgar) pains in the butt; people who are being deliberately annoying

SOLICITOR lawyer

STONE measurement of weight, approximately 14 pounds

SUSSED (colloq.) knowledgeable

TAKE-AWAY take-out

TALKING CLOCK telephone service that gives the time of day

TATE MODERN gallery of modern art in London

TELLY (abbr.) television

TENNER (colloq.) ten-pound note

TERM school semester

TINNED, TIN canned, can

TORY member of the Conservative Party

TRAINERS sneakers

TROLLEY shopping cart

TUBE London subway

V very

V&A (abbr.) Victoria and Albert Museum

VEGGIE vegetarian

WARDROBE external closet

WASHING POWDER detergent

WATER BISCUITS thin, plain crackers

WELL (colloq.) very

WELLIES high, waterproof rubber boots; also called Wellingtons

WICKED (colloq.) cool

WIND UP push one's buttons

WOBBLY (colloq.) tantrum

WOOLIE'S (colloq.) affectionate term for Woolworth's, a chain of five-and-dime stores that no longer operates in the U.S. but is still in business in the U.K.

YORKSHIRE PUDDING similar to a popover, baked either muffin style or in a flat pan; traditionally served with roast beef